Daniel returned with two [illegible] glasses of ice water. As the water wet her lips, she battled what she'd been battling all day: the desire to kiss him.

"Are you scared?" he asked.

"Yes." But not just of the stalker. She was afraid of the constant hunger, too.

"I'll keep you safe, Allie. I swear I will."

"I know. I trust you."

"If you have trouble sleeping tonight, you can come to my room."

The glass almost slipped from her hand. "You're inviting me to sleep with you?"

"Not with me. Beside me. We won't do anything."

"We won't?" This was the strangest conversation she'd ever had.

"No. I mean, we can control our urges." He searched her expression. "Right?"

Did he need to prove that they could keep their relationship at a no-sex level, even if they shared the same bed? Was that why he'd made the offer? Or was he truly worried about her being alone, steeped in stalker nightmares? She suspected it was a combination of both.

Dear Reader,

This story has been a long time coming. Allie Whirlwind and Daniel Deer Runner appeared in *Never Look Back,* my 2006 Silhouette Bombshell. Since then, I've received numerous e-mails about them. Readers kept asking if their romance was going to continue. You see, at the end of *Never Look Back,* Allie had just sent her former lover to the Apache Underworld, and Daniel, the WARRIOR SOCIETY member who saved her life, was awakening from a coma.

So here it is....

Imminent Affair.

For those of you who remember Allie and Daniel, this book is for you. For those of you who haven't met them yet, this book is also for you. Within the pages of *Imminent Affair,* Allie and Daniel enter a new phase of their lives. Dangerous, yes, but loving, too. Which is, after all, the wonder and beauty of romantic suspense.

Love,

Sheri WhiteFeather

SHERI
WHITEFEATHER

Imminent Affair

Recycling programs for this product may not exist in your area.

ISBN-13: 978-0-373-27656-1

IMMINENT AFFAIR

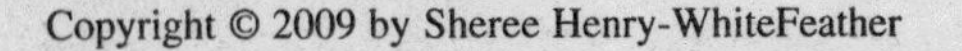

This edition published by arrangement with Harlequin Books S.A.

Visit Silhouette Books at www.eHarlequin.com

Printed in U.S.A.

Books by Sheri WhiteFeather

Silhouette Romantic Suspense

Mob Mistress #1469
Killer Passion #1520
**Imminent Affair* #1586

Silhouette Desire

Sleeping With Her Rival #1496
Cherokee Baby #1509
Cherokee Dad #1523
The Heart of a Stranger #1527
Cherokee Stranger #1563
A Kept Woman #1575
Steamy Savannah Nights #1597
Betrayed Birthright #1663
Apache Nights #1678
Expecting Thunder's Baby #1742
Marriage of Revenge #1751
The Morning-After Proposal #1756

*Warrior Society

Silhouette Bombshell

Always Look Twice #27
Never Look Back #84

SHERI WHITEFEATHER

pens a variety of romances for Silhouette Books. She has earned several prestigious readers' and reviewers' choice awards and become known for incorporating Native American elements into her stories.

Sheri's hobbies include decorating with antiques and shopping in thrift stores for vintage clothes. Currently, she lives in a cowboy community in Central Valley, California.

She loves to hear from her readers. To contact Sheri, visit her Web site at www.SheriWhiteFeather.com.

Chapter 1

Allie Whirlwind couldn't breathe. The air in her lungs wouldn't expel. She felt as if someone were sitting on her chest, forcing her to relive a nightmare.

Only this nightmare didn't involve her serial killer mother or her psychic sister or the ghost of her father. It didn't involve Raven, either. Her former shape-shifter lover had moved on to the underworld, to an Apache place that rivaled heaven.

And now Allie was in hell.

While she'd been at work, someone had come into her loft and trashed her bedroom. Just moments ago, she'd opened the door and encountered the gruesome sight.

Her sheets had been slashed. The canopy above

her bed had been knifed. On the wall nearest the window, red paint dripped like blood, with a message in the center that said This is for Daniel.

Still struggling to breathe, she stared at the elegantly scripted letters. The vandal had used a lovely form of calligraphy. Daniel's name was especially pretty.

This is for Daniel.

What was? The mock blood? The knifed anger? The whole chilling scene?

Was Daniel in danger? Panicked, she reached for the phone and dialed his cell.

He answered on the second ring, apparently recognizing her number from caller ID. "Hey, Allie."

The air in her lungs finally whooshed out. He was the man she loved, but she didn't have the courage to tell him. As far as he knew, she simply regarded him as a friend. But that was all he considered her, too. He didn't remember that deeper feelings had developed between them. Daniel Deer Runner had retrograde amnesia.

"Allie?" he addressed her again, filling the silence.

"I'm so glad you're all right," she said.

"Why wouldn't I be? I'm on a break at work." He paused for a second. "What's going on? Are *you* okay?"

She bit back a rush of tears. "Someone slashed up my bedroom and used red paint that looks like blood. They left a message that said they did it for you."

His voice went anxiety-ridden gruff. "Someone? Someone who?"

"I don't know."

"Did you call the police?"

"Yes." She'd done that right away.

"Good. Stay put, and I'll be there as soon as I can."

Oh, thank God, she thought. He was coming over. They hung up, and she waited in the living room, with Christmas decorations twinkling in every corner. This was Allie's favorite time of year.

Clinging to her holiday spirit, she lit some cookie-scented candles, hoping that Daniel would get there before the LAPD.

No such luck.

The police arrived in record time. Most local cops knew her, or at least knew of her. She was even friends with some of the Special Sections homicide detectives. But these detectives were unfamiliar, and that did little to steady her nerves. Being the daughter of a serial killer made Allie and her sister uncomfortably famous. Not only was their mother a murderer, she was a black magic witch, and in their culture, witchcraft was evil. The question, "Are you a good witch or a bad witch?" didn't apply. But at least Mom was in prison now, paying her debt to society on death row.

A detective named Bell interviewed Allie. He was tall and blond and purposely expressionless. They went into her bedroom and stood amid the mess.

"Who's Daniel?" he asked, scribbling on a notepad and glancing up at the message on the wall. His partner did other investigative-type things, like interviewing neighbors, taking photographs of the vandalism, checking for signs of forced entry and dusting for prints.

"He's a friend," she responded, wishing that Daniel didn't make her ache. Allie had always dreamed of falling in love, but not with a man whose lack of memory robbed her of a future with him. "He's on his way. He should be here soon."

Bell merely nodded. "Does anyone else live here?"

"Not anymore. My sister used to, but she just got married. She's in Europe on her honeymoon. Her husband is a special agent. You know. FBI."

No visible reaction, aside from another nod.

Allie fidgeted with the silver beads around her neck. She favored Native jewelry and wore it often. She was a full-blood from the Oglala Lakota Sioux and Chiricahua Apache Nations.

"He saved my life," she heard herself say. Her mind was moving in what seemed like a zillion different directions. She hadn't meant to offer unsolicited information.

"The special agent?"

She shook her head. "Daniel."

That got Bell's attention. He exhibited a genuinely interested expression. "How?"

"He stepped in front of a loaded gun that was aimed at me." Just in case the officer presumed that the message on the wall was related to the shooting, she explained that the shooter, an admirer of her mother's, was in prison now and was no longer a threat.

"How badly was Daniel hit?"

"Bad enough to need surgery, to slip into a coma and lose most of his memory."

"Which means what? That he won't be able to provide answers as to who might've done this and why?"

"Probably not. But he'll do his damnedest to try." Daniel Deer Runner belonged to a Warrior Society, a group of former military men who excelled at close quarter combat and fought for Native causes. He wouldn't let something like this go. He wouldn't let someone torment Allie in his name.

Anxious to see him, she fidgeted with her jewelry again. Daniel consumed her mind far more often than he should.

He arrived a few minutes later, cradling Samantha. Sam was Allie's cat, a fussy black stray that shunned almost everyone except Allie. Sam adored Daniel, but he'd worked on wooing her.

"I found her outside," he said. "She was hiding under the stoop. The vandal must have scared her."

He handed Allie the cat, and when she took Samantha, their hands connected. Touching him was almost more than she could bear. She wanted to wrap her arms around him, to take comfort in his strength.

Daniel stood tall and broad, with medium-length, slightly messy black hair and killer cheekbones. He used to iron his jeans, slick back his hair and sport horn-rimmed glasses. But he'd changed since the coma. He'd ditched his ironing board, traded his glasses for contact lenses and tossed out the Brylcreem.

Today he wore dark blue scrubs. He was a veterinary technician at the zoo, and although he struggled to recall people from his past, he clearly remembered how to do his job.

"I'm sorry this is happening to you," he said. "That someone…" He frowned at his name on the wall.

Allie couldn't seem to find her voice. Detective Bell stood back, watching her and Daniel. Did the cop suspect how she felt about her "friend?" Did the person who'd vandalized Allie's room suspect it, too? Was that a key point? Was the vandal another woman who had designs on Daniel?

He reached out and skimmed the side of her arm, and the long, gentle stroke from his fingers gave her soft, sexy chills.

"You're so quiet," he said.

She tightened her hold on the squirming cat. Apparently Sam wanted to bolt, to hide under the stoop again. Or maybe she wanted to climb back into Daniel's protective arms. Allie certainly understood that.

Since he was waiting for a response, she said, "I should be used to creepy things by now. But coming home to this was shocking." Mostly because it was related to him. The creepiness from the past had involved her mother.

Daniel frowned at the wall again, and Detective Bell led him away from Allie to interview him. She remained off to the side, noticing that Bell was more cordial with Daniel than he had been with her.

The boy's club, she thought. It made her feel like a third wheel. But she supposed that sweetening the loft with cookie-scented candles made her seem like a girly-girl, which she was, most of the time. Sometimes she even got lost in her own dreams. Allie was a fantasy artist who painted sensual mermaids, fire-breathing dragons and castles in the sky. For her day job, she gave art lessons at a bustling senior citizen community center.

Not that Allie wasn't trained in self defense or couldn't hold her own. Of course the last time she was in danger, Daniel had taken a bullet for her. She hadn't done a very good job of protecting herself.

Bell ended the interview, and Daniel returned to her.

"I want you to come home with me," he said. "To stay at my house until this is over."

She looked into his eyes and noticed that the light caught a corner of his contact lenses. Two months had passed since he'd lost his memory, since Daniel had morphed into a harder-edged man, and she was still getting used to the alpha he'd become. Although he'd always been tall and muscular with striking features, he'd also been a bit of a nerd, even to the Warrior Society. Years ago, they'd nicknamed him "Fearless" derived from Fearless Fly, a goofy vintage cartoon character that obtained superpowers from his glasses.

Sometimes Allie missed Daniel's glasses. Sometimes she missed who he used to be. But the new Daniel was wildly compelling, and she couldn't help but love him, too. He was Fearless either way. The nickname still fit.

A scowl bracketed his mouth. "Why aren't you talking to me, Allie?"

Oh, damn. She'd done it again. She'd kept quiet. "I'm not sure about going home with you."

The scowl deepened. "Why not?"

Because sleeping under the same roof would only make her want him that much more. She fabricated an excuse. "My studio is here."

"I have a couple of extra rooms. You can use one of them as a studio."

She put Sam on the ground. The cat was meowing for her freedom. "I know, but—"

"But nothing. I'm not leaving you here alone. Detective Bell thinks this could turn into a stalking, and I agree. We think the vandal is a deranged woman from my past who considers your friendship with me a threat."

Allie had already mulled over that possibility. The calligraphy seemed deliberately feminine, as if the vandal was identifying herself as a woman, especially from the pretty way she'd written Daniel's name. "How did she get into my loft?"

"The front door lock was picked. But that isn't a complicated lock. A credit card would have done the trick."

"Maybe the police will come up with some fingerprints."

"Maybe, but it's doubtful. More than likely, she was wearing gloves."

"How many deranged women from your past do you think are out there?"

He tunneled his hands through his already messy

hair. "How the hell would I know? I'm going to ask Rex Sixkiller to investigate my life, the things I can't remember."

"Is Rex from the Warrior Society?"

"Yes, but he's a licensed P.I., too."

She could only imagine how invasive for Daniel that was going to be. "What about Glynis?"

He squinted. "Who?"

"Glynis Mitchell. She's a former lover of yours, and a bit of an enemy of mine. She's never done anything threatening, but she disliked me from the start."

Daniel cocked his head. "Because of me?"

"Because of my mother. A lot of people dislike me for being related to Yvonne Whirlwind." A connection that made Allie sick, too. "Still, I should probably tell Bell about Glynis."

"Yes, you definitely should." He angled his head again. "Why didn't you ever mention her to me before?"

Allie shrugged, trying to seem more unaffected than she was. She didn't like thinking about Daniel with other women. "Glynis didn't seem to matter until now."

"After you talk to Bell, you need to pack your bags," he said, reminding her that he wasn't taking no for an answer. She was going home with him, whether she wanted to or not.

While Allie settled into a guest room at his house, Daniel waited for her to join him in the kitchen for dinner. He wasn't much of a cook, and since Allie was a vegetarian, he tossed a simple green salad and proceeded to grill a couple of cheese sandwiches. He put on a pot of herbal tea, too. Allie liked hot tea.

Samantha purred at his feet and he reached down to pet her, but the cat wouldn't be staying for very long. Tomorrow, she would be going to a boarding facility. Allie was worried that Sam might become the target of the vandal's next threat, and Daniel agreed that it was a valid concern.

He petted Sam again, thinking how pretty she was, much like her mistress. Allie was a bit of cat herself. Long, lean and feline.

Damn, Daniel thought. *Damn.*

Allie stirred a blood-burning hunger he was desperately trying to suppress. Being friends with a woman that you wanted to strip naked wasn't a good thing.

To make matters worse, he couldn't remember the last time he'd gotten laid, and he meant that literally. He'd been celibate since the post-surgical coma that had wiped out most of his memory.

She entered the kitchen, and his pulse quickened. She looked so soft, so beautiful, so vulnerable, he battled his emotions. Beyond the attraction was an overwhelming desire to keep her safe.

The scene at her loft had knotted his gut. If it went further, if someone tried to harm her…

"I think it's done," she said.

He gave her a blank stare. Or maybe it wasn't so blank. At the moment, he'd become fixated on her waist-length hair, on the way it framed her face and wrapped her in flowing lines. "I'm sorry. What?"

"That sandwich. You're killing it."

He glanced down at the pan. He was squishing the grilled bread with a spatula, making cheese leak out the sides. He scooped it up and put it on a plate, then realized how unattractive the presentation was. Trying to pretty it up, he reached for shiny red apple from a basket on the counter and placed it beside the sandwich. He'd already put the salad on the table.

Once both plates were fixed, he and Allie sat down to eat. She didn't seem to mind his lousy cooking. Either that or she was too hungry to care. The tea seemed to help, too. She sweetened it with honey and sipped generously.

"Tell me more about Glynis," he said. It was odd to ask one woman about another, but what else could he do? He had no recollection of his former lover. His doctor claimed that portions of his memory might return, but a full recovery was doubtful.

Allie glanced up from her plate. "She owns a string of mortuaries that she inherited from her late husband. She's always had a 'thing' for death."

Daniel made a tight face. If Glynis was the vandal, she might be capable of anything. Not only that, but why would he have slept with a woman who was intrigued by death? That didn't bode well for his character.

"In the eighties, she ran a Death Rock club," Allie said.

"The eighties?" Not only did Glynis sound odd, she was older than he'd expected. "I dated a cougar?"

"That's one way of putting it, I guess. But I can see why you were attracted to her. She's quite glamorous. She resembles Bettie Page."

"The 1950s pinup model?" Daniel got an image of a shapely brunette wearing fetish gear. The Glynis scenario was getting weirder. He wondered what sort of relationship he'd had with her. He couldn't begin to describe how disturbing it was not knowing intimate details about himself.

He quit eating. The sandwich tasted like crap anyway. "I wasn't into kinky sex, was I?"

Caught off guard, Allie coughed on a sip of tea, and he realized how inappropriate the question was. He couldn't backpedal, so he apologized. "I'm sorry. I wouldn't expect you to know something like that."

Her cheeks turned rosy, making her look young and sweet, even if she was almost thirty.

Daniel discarded his kinky sex concerns. He might be lusting after Allie, but he wasn't envisioning her in a rubber corset and bondage ties. He would rather see her in a luxurious nightgown, something long and lacy.

He wanted to reach across the table and touch her, but he resumed their conversation, returning to Glynis. "What does her fascination with death entail?"

"When she was younger, she used to pen pal with killers on death row. After she met her husband, she learned to respect death the way he did, not wallow in the morbid side of it. Or that's what she claimed."

"Do you know how I got hooked up with her?"

"Her husband supported the Native American Graves and Repatriation Act. He helped the Warrior Society recover stolen remains and funerary objects to their rightful owners."

"So I knew him?"

"Yes, and after he died, you helped Glynis get through her grief."

By sleeping with her? Daniel frowned. "That doesn't make me sound very honorable."

"You were honorable to me." Her gaze locked onto his, and a blast of emotion erupted between them. "You saved my life. You…" Her voice broke, making the connection between them even more sensitive.

"I don't remember the shooting."

Her voice rattled some more. "I remember for both of us."

"Remembering for me doesn't count." He wanted his own memories.

She didn't say anything, and when things got too uncomfortable, he cleared the table. She'd eaten all of her food, lousy as it was.

He turned to look at her. "I think you should take some time off. Maybe call in sick, then arrange for a vacation or whatever." He would be taking time away from his job, as well. "Tomorrow we can meet with Rex and get started on the investigation. We can pay Glynis a visit, too."

"She won't like us dropping by."

"Too bad for her." He wasn't leaving any stone

unturned, regardless of where it led or what it revealed about his past.

He was going to protect Allie. Every shaky step of the way.

Chapter 2

Later that night Allie got ready for bed. She rummaged through her nightgowns and pajamas, contemplating what to wear. Not that it mattered. Daniel wasn't going to see her. He'd already retired to his room.

Still, having him so close, so heart-flutteringly near, she couldn't resist the urge to look pretty, to feel pretty, to don something soft and feminine. She went for a classic silk nightgown with a hint of ribbon and lace. The champagne-colored fabric hugged her curves and flowed at the hemline.

She washed her face and removed her makeup, then brushed her hair until it shined. The ends skimmed her tailbone.

Okay. There. She looked good. She felt good.

Allie scooted into bed and got restless. Being pretty for herself wasn't enough.

She wanted to see Daniel, and she wanted him to see her. *So do it,* her mind coaxed. *Find an excuse to knock on his door.*

What excuse? That there were monsters under her bed?

The thought made her smile. At one time, she had endured monsters. Real ones. Allie's diabolical ancestors had conjured witchcraft creatures, and she and Daniel had battled them. He'd helped her through the most difficult time of her life.

Was it any wonder that she loved him?

She got out of bed and checked her appearance in the mirror, giving her hair one final fluff and her nightgown one last body-clinging smooth. From there, she ventured into the hallway. Daniel lived in a modest North Hollywood residence, but he'd fixed it up nicely. He'd made all sorts of improvements, including new carpets, new floors and landscaping the front and back yards. In return, the landlord had discounted his rent.

Allie paused outside his room. A small strip of light shimmered beneath his door, a telltale sign that he remained awake. She still hadn't come up with an excuse to be visiting him at this hour. But she knocked anyway. She was good at thinking on her feet.

He called out from behind the wooden barrier, "Come in."

Suddenly she was nervous. She wanted to turn tail and run, but it was too late for that.

Allie opened the door and entered his room. He was sitting on the edge of his bed, with a paperback on the nightstand. His chest was bare, making the scar from his surgery visible, and he wore drawstring pajama bottoms slung low on his hips. She glanced at his navel and his gloriously rippled abs. Before she looked too hard and too deep, she shifted her attention to his face.

He was checking her out, too. His dark gaze slid up and down her nightgown-clad body and rested momentarily on her breasts. She prayed that her nipples didn't get hard. Self-consciousness was setting in. But so was a major revelation.

Although Daniel treated her like a friend, he was sexually attracted to her. Some of what he'd felt for her prior to the coma was still there, sluicing through his blood. If Allie wasn't such a Chicken Little, she could seduce him.

Climb right in his lap and make him moan.

"What's going on?" he finally asked.

"Nothing. I just wanted to say goodnight." So much for thinking on her feet. They'd already bid each other goodnight earlier.

He stood up, and his height dwarfed the military-tidy room. "Are you having trouble sleeping?"

"A little."

"So am I. But I'm a bit of an insomniac anyway." He adjusted the waistband of his pajama bottoms, lifting them a smidgen. They'd fallen even lower on his hips. "Was I always?"

God, he looked gorgeous. Rough and ready. "Were you always what?"

"An insomniac?"

She tried not to stammer. He was moving closer. "I don't know. We never slept near each other."

"But we fought paranormal creatures, searched for a magic talisman and helped your cursed lover get back to his dead wife?"

"It sounds unbelievable, but that's what we did." Her cursed lover had been a time-traveling warrior who'd shape-shifted into a raven.

"Was it hard to let him go?"

The question threw her. Daniel had never questioned her in detail about Raven. "I wanted him to be happy, to find peace." Before Raven went away, he'd asked Daniel to look after her. But since Daniel didn't remember, she wasn't about to tell him. There was only so much she could say about the past without getting emotional. Besides, he *was* looking after her, even without recalling his promise to Raven.

Allie shifted her bare feet. By now, she and Daniel stood face-to-face. Seducing him crossed her mind again, but she thought better of it. She wanted more from him than sex. She wanted him to remember that he'd loved her.

He had loved her, hadn't he? He'd never come right out and said it, but she assumed that he had.

A knot grew in her belly. What if she'd been wrong? What if all he'd ever felt for her was a physical attraction?

She glanced at the neon green numbers on the alarm clock. It was almost midnight, and she was battling a newfound blast of anxiety. "I should go. I should try to get some sleep."

"Me, too. For all the good it will do." He reached out to touch a spaghetti strap on her nightgown. "You look pretty, Allie."

The knot in her stomach got tighter. Was he making a play for her?

"I imagined you wearing something like this. If I didn't know better, I'd say you wore it on purpose." He snared her gaze. "You're not psychic, are you? Like your sister?"

She felt like a rabbit caught in a trap. "I can't read people's minds. And you shouldn't have been thinking about me in my bedclothes."

"The way you shouldn't be coming to my room looking like an innocent siren?" He stepped back, putting distance between them. He wasn't making a play. He was reprimanding her, along with himself. "We're both guilty of misconduct."

Yes, they were, and he was too damn observant for his own good. Struggling to temper her emotions, she said good-night once again, and turned and left his room, closing the door gently behind her.

Too bad he wasn't observant enough to figure out that the innocent siren loved him.

* * *

The sun shone through the windows, making Daniel aware of its yellow rays. Christmas was only two weeks away, but the Southern California weather didn't seem to know the difference. Not that Daniel cared. The holidays didn't make him cheerful. Why he felt like a bit of a Scrooge, he couldn't say. But lots of people got depressed around Christmas, so he tried not to make too much of it.

Although he was still sleep deprived, he showered, shaved, and donned a pair of freshly laundered jeans and a basic white T-shirt. Next, he headed to the kitchen where Allie was getting a jumpstart on breakfast. She'd already beaten him to the punch and brewed a pot of coffee, and now she was cracking eggs into a bowl.

He stood in the doorway and watched her. She was wearing a big, fluffy pink robe and ugly slippers with mottled colors. He assumed that the pretty nightgown was underneath, but damn if he could tell. She was belted good and tight. He supposed that after last night's encounter, she wasn't taking any chances. But at least it was out in the open. At least they'd admitted that they were attracted to each other. Or sort of admitted it. Whatever the case, one thing was clear: they weren't going to act on it.

Maintaining a platonic relationship was best. Safer, he thought. Less complicated.

"Morning," he said by way of a greeting.

She glanced up, and they stared at each other,

trapped in remnants of the awkward stuff. He cursed the caveman feeling that being near her gave him. He wanted to toss her over his shoulder and carry her back to his bed, ugly robe and all.

Finally, she gestured to the food on the counter. She'd diced onions and tomatoes to go along with the eggs. She'd grated cheddar cheese, too. "I hope you don't mind that I raided your fridge."

"No, it's fine. Help yourself. You're a far better cook than I am." But who wasn't?

"Do you want an omelet?"

"I'd love one. Could you put ham in mine, though?" He wasn't up for another meatless meal. The awful sandwich from yesterday hadn't stuck to his ribs. He needed something with substance.

She opened the refrigerator to get the ham, and Daniel walked past her to pour himself some coffee. He took a closer look at her slippers and noticed that they were cat faces, with pointed ears, plastic eyeballs, tiny pom-pom noses and long white whiskers.

He couldn't help but smile. They were even more ridiculous than he'd first assumed. He pointed to the fur balls in question. "Does Sam like those?"

"She loves them." Allie wiggled her feet. "So do I."

"It must be a girl thing."

"I suppose you think they're atrocious."

"Yeah, but it's okay. You can wear whatever you want." Except pretty nightgowns while she was in his room. He made a show of looking around. "By the way, where is Sam?"

"She was up earlier, but she went back to sleep."

In Allie's soft, warm bed, no doubt. "I guess she's not an insomniac."

"No. She's a cozy sleeper. But cats are supposed to take catnaps."

Daniel's omelet was done first. Somewhere in the midst of their conversation, Allie managed to fix hash browns, too. She handed him his food, and he stood near the sink and wolfed it down. He didn't sit at the table because he didn't want to make a domestic ritual out of sharing meals with her. It was bad enough that he'd brought her to his house for an extended stay.

But what choice did he have? The vandal, the potential stalker, was all too real, and he intended to do whatever it took to keep Allie safe.

Would he take another bullet for her? Yeah, he thought, he would. He would do just about anything for Allie Whirlwind. He wasn't sure why; he just knew that he would.

"You're going to get heartburn." She scolded him for eating so fast.

"I'm fine." To prove his point, he took a second helping of hashed browns.

She shook her head and sat at the table, spreading a napkin on her lap. She would have looked quite proper if it weren't for the horrendous robe and slippers.

"I already called Rex," he said. "He'll be here in a few hours."

"I wonder where he'll start."

"With my background, I suppose."

"Are you nervous about it?"

"Why?" He scooped the last of his food onto his fork. "Do you think I have something to hide?"

"No. I just can't imagine being in your position."

"I can't imagine being in yours, either."

"Getting my loft trashed or having the kind of ancestors that I do?"

"Both." He thought Allie was too sweet to hail from a lineage of evil witches, but that was her background, her burden to bear. He had no idea what his was going to be.

He'd lied about not being nervous.

By the time Rex arrived, Daniel's anxiety was at an all-time high. But he hid his feelings, greeting the other man with a sturdy handshake and inviting him into the living room.

Rex Sixkiller was a half-blood from the Cherokee Nation. At thirty-six, he was the same age as Daniel, and although they weren't from the same unit, they were both Desert Storm veterans who had served in the army. But like most people from Daniel's past, he had no recollection of Rex. Of course since regaining consciousness, Daniel had made a point of spending time with the Warrior Society, and that included Rex.

"Where's Allie?" the P.I. asked.

"In her room. I'll go get her."

Daniel went down the hall and knocked on her door. She appeared in a colorful Santa Fe style dress and a pair of western boots. Her hair was plaited in a single braid that hung down her back, leaving the angles of her beautifully sculpted face unframed. Her earrings were big silver hoops decorated with turquoise nuggets.

"Rex is here," he said.

"Oh, okay. I'm ready."

She walked beside him, and upon entering the living room, Daniel made the introduction. Rex rose to meet her. He also checked her out a bit too closely, putting Daniel on edge. From what he knew, Rex was single and somewhat of a player.

Daniel gave his comrade a territorial stare, and Rex looked back at him with a curious expression. Apparently the other man had wanted to gauge Daniel's reaction, to see what he and Allie were truly about. And now he knew.

Daniel had the hots for his female friend.

"Let's get started," Rex said, settling back onto the sofa and elbowing a leopard-print pillow.

Daniel sat next to him, leaving a leather recliner for Allie.

For a moment, they were all silent, then Rex turned to Daniel and said, "Tell me what you recall from your past."

"I recall bits and pieces about my parents. My dad lives close by, and my mom died when I was a boy. I'm from the Lakota and Haida Nations."

"Do you remember being from those tribes or is that something you were told after the coma?"

"I remember." He paused, then frowned. "I also

remember Mom's body being laid out at the funeral house. It isn't a good memory."

"No. I don't suppose it is." Rex furrowed his brows. "Do you have any good memories?"

"Not really." Daniel paused once again, pondering the question. "Actually, my memories of Allie are good."

He glanced her way, and she scooted to the edge of the recliner. As soon as their gazes locked, he broke eye contact. He wasn't comfortable with Rex watching.

"How good are they?" the P.I. asked, almost making the query sound like a double entendre.

Not that good, Daniel wanted to say. "They're kind of warm and fuzzy, I guess." He hoped that didn't sound stupid, but it was the only description that came to mind. "I don't remember her as much as the feeling of being around her."

"And it was warm and fuzzy?"

"For lack of a better term, yeah."

Rex shifted his attention to Allie. "Does that sound about right to you?"

She nodded. "Daniel and I were close."

"But there was no romance?"

"No." She started to fidget.

Annoyed, Daniel squinted at the P.I. "Is this line of questioning necessary?"

"Yes, it is. I need to know if there's anything that happened between the two of you that the vandal might have seen or heard." Rex pushed Allie a little further. "No romance at all?"

"No," she said again.

"Not even one little oops? One little kiss?"

She responded with another fidgety, "No."

Rex kept pushing. "Were you visibly attracted to each other? The way you are now?" he added, not mincing his observations or his words.

Her breath hitched. "Yes."

Damn, Daniel thought. This hungry-for-each-other thing wasn't new. He gave Rex a flustered stare. "Can we move on now?"

Rex gave him a tight nod in return. "Yes, but I'd like to know about other women from your past. Do you recall any of your former lovers?"

"No, and I already told you about Glynis over the phone."

"She's a good place to start, but she can't be the only significant woman from your past. I'm going to have to interview your friends and family and see what they know."

"You're an old friend," Daniel pointed out. "Don't you remember me being with anyone?"

"Unfortunately I don't. You were private that way. But someone else from The Society might have a helpful recollection."

Having his life dissected by other people sucked, Daniel thought. "What if the vandal isn't a former lover? What if it's someone with a whacked-out crush on me?"

"I plan to work on that angle, too. And I'm going to need as much cooperation as I can get from you."

He looked at Allie. "And from you. Whoever did this has probably been watching you and Daniel. Tracking your relationship. She might even blame you for his memory loss."

Daniel spoke up. "You'll get our cooperation. But I'm not sitting idly by. This is my investigation, too. Whatever leads you uncover, or the police discover, or I find out on my own, I'm following through on them. I'm doing the legwork."

"I figured you would." A second later, Rex addressed Allie, including her once again. "And you, too. From what I heard, you and Fearless made quite a team."

"We did," she admitted softly, drawing Daniel to the sound of her voice, to that warm and fuzzy feeling that lingered in his scattered mind.

Chapter 3

Allie rode beside Daniel in his truck. That was another thing about him that had changed. He used to drive a simple white van, but he'd traded it in for a sleek black pickup with custom wheels and tires.

Allie had never liked the van, anyway. His new vehicle was much sexier. But so was he. Everything about him left her breathless. She glanced at his profile and got warm and tingly.

"You okay?" he asked.

"Why? Don't I seem all right?"

"You're fussing with your seat belt."

Because the device seemed too tight across her Daniel-deprived body. One little kiss, one little oops, as Rex had put it, sounded darn good about now. "I'm okay."

"Are you nervous about seeing Glynis?"

Allie glanced out the window. They'd just dropped off Sam at the veterinary clinic where she would be boarded, and now they were headed to Daniel's old lover's house.

"Are you?" he asked again.

"Yes," she responded truthfully. She'd never expected to confront his ex again. She'd had enough run-ins with Glynis in the past to last a lifetime.

"I can take you back to my place," he offered. "I can do this alone."

"No way." Allie wanted to see the other woman's reaction firsthand. "I wonder if we'll be able to tell if she's the vandal, if she'll give herself away."

"That seems doubtful. From what you said about her, she sounds complex."

"She is. I was hoping this would be easy, I guess."

Daniel turned onto Ventura Boulevard, following the directions Allie had given him earlier. "Can you still paint magic pictures?"

The question caused her to widen her eyes. "Do you remember that about me?"

He shook his head. "You told me about it."

"Oh, that's right, I did."

"Well, can you?"

"I don't know." Her experience with Raven had started with a portrait she'd painted of him. "I haven't been involved in anything magical since then."

"What about sensing the presence of ghosts? Can you still do that?"

Once again, she didn't know. "I suppose I could if there was a ghost who insinuated itself into our lives." Last time, both she and Daniel had made contact with ghosts, but her connection to the spiritual world had been stronger than his. "Why? Are you getting a ghostly vibe?"

"No, but I feel kind of sad." He stared out the windshield. "And it feels like a memory." He shot her a quick glance. "How bizarre is that?"

She sat up a little straighter, stretching her too-tight seat belt. "The doctor said you'd probably regain bits and pieces of your memory."

"I know. But I wasn't expecting this."

"Tell me exactly what you're feeling."

"That someone who mattered to me died. Someone besides my mom."

"A woman? A lover?"

"A teenage girl, I think. But the vandal isn't a ghost. Whoever trashed your room was a real person. A ghost wouldn't have picked the lock."

She couldn't imagine a ghost slashing her bedding with a knife or using blood-red paint, either. But Daniel's sudden sadness gave her pause. "You should tell Rex."

"I will. After all of the paranormal stuff that happened before, we can't be too careful."

"I agree." She sighed, wondering if there really was a ghost in their midst. She didn't feel anything, but maybe her supernatural skills were gone. Or maybe she only felt ghosts that were connected to her, and this one belonged to Daniel.

He drove the rest of the way without sparking another conversation, frowning at the road. Allie didn't talk, either. She couldn't think of anything pertinent to say.

Finally he turned onto Glynis's street, and Allie directed him to her house. He parked at the curb.

"Is that her car?" he asked, pointing to the silver Mercedes in the circular driveway.

Allie nodded. Daniel's former bedmate lived in a Tuscan estate in Studio City with a spectacular view. She had lots of money and lots of style. Women like Glynis Mitchell ruled the San Fernando Valley.

They took the flagstone path that led to the front door. Exotic plants bloomed in artfully tended flower beds and heart-shaped ivy crept along the building and up around the windows, where rustic shutters were drawn tight.

Allie rang the bell, and the housekeeper, a short, stout woman with graying hair, answered the summons and spurned them with a bitter look. She was fiercely loyal to her employer and had given Allie trouble before.

Daniel gazed at her as if she were supposed to be Glynis. "She doesn't look like Bettie Page to me."

Allie bit back a smile. He knew darn well that this snippy old broad wasn't his former lover.

The housekeeper raised her eyebrows at him, but

whether she was reacting to his smart-aleck remark or to the obvious changes in his appearance was unclear. "What do you two want?"

"We'd like to see Glynis," Allie responded.

"Mrs. Mitchell is relaxing."

With a martini, Allie thought. Oh, wait. Glynis favored a cocktail called Vampire's Kiss. That was her drink of choice.

"We're not going away," Daniel said. "So you may as well tell her that we're on her doorstep."

The housekeeper stormed off in a huff.

She came back a few seconds later and pointed a crooked finger at Daniel, explaining why they were being allowed admittance. "Mrs. Mitchell is curious to see you."

From there, she ushered them into the living room and said, "Wait here."

Daniel glanced around, but Allie didn't need to take in her surroundings. The house looked the same.

The décor presented mottled colors with terra cotta accents. The floors were brick, and the furniture was constructed of timeworn woods. Glynis's late husband had collected Native American artifacts, and the stunning collection included tribal masks, baskets, pottery, small stone carvings and arrowheads. Strings of chevron beads, probably dating back to Christopher Columbus's time, were displayed in glass cases.

Holiday decorations dazzled the interior, as well. An artificial Christmas tree shimmered with white lights and crystal ornaments.

"Well, now..." A luxuriously feminine voice sounded from the living room entryway.

Allie and Daniel spun around. There stood Glynis in all of her aging-siren glory. Her pinup-girl hairdo was perfectly coiffed with short rolled bangs and flowing, dark locks. She wore capri pants, high heels and a feather-trimmed blouse. Although she was in her early fifties, she had the figure of someone much, much younger. But didn't most rich L.A. women? They bought themselves boobs, got liposuction if they gained an ounce of fat and did Pilates with private trainers.

Daniel stared at her, and she stared back at him.

Uncomfortable, Allie sucked in a silent breath.

Finally he said to Glynis, "I don't remember you."

"Yes, I heard that you had amnesia." Her glossy red lips curved into a deliberate smile. "It's been a long while since we dated, but I'd be glad to refresh your memory."

"I'll bet you would." He kept his expression blank. "But my tastes have changed."

"Oh, that's right. You have a crush on Allie. I noticed it the last time I saw you together, before the amnesia and all that." Glynis finally turned to face her rival. "Have you let him into your pants yet? Or are you still being a tease?"

Before Allie could respond, Daniel snapped at Glynis. "Don't talk to her like that."

The other woman kept her cool. "I guess that means she's still being a tease. Poor boy. That's what you get for falling for a witch."

Allie came to her own defense. "I'm not a witch."

"You're not evil like your mother? I wonder if it's possible to have those genes and not be just a little bit evil."

Allie narrowed her eyes. Was Glynis the vandal? Was she behaving like a potential stalker? Or just a jealous old girlfriend?

"So what's going on?" Glynis asked, switching tactics. "Why did you stop by?"

"To harass you," Allie said in her drollest tone.

"Very funny. What for?"

"As if you don't know."

"Please, no games. Just tell me what this is about."

"Someone broke into Allie's loft and trashed her bedroom," Daniel said.

Much too dramatic, Glynis clutched a hand to her blouse, ruffling the boa-type feathers. Her fingernails were as red as her lips. "And you think it was me?"

"It seems like a possibility."

"I wouldn't waste my time."

"Wouldn't you?" he challenged. "Not even for me?"

"No, dear boy. That isn't my style. But feel free to give my regards to whoever did it."

"Any idea who that could be?" Cynicism edged his voice. "Besides you?"

"If you're asking me who else you slept with, I have no idea. You weren't the type to kiss and tell. Speaking of kisses, why don't we have a drink?"

He furrowed his brow. Apparently he wasn't following Glynis's logic. Allie was, but she remained silent.

He asked, "What do drinks have to do with kisses?"

"Oh, that's right. You don't remember. I have a Vampire's Kiss every day. Sometimes you had one with me. But mostly you preferred Gin and Nothing."

"I'll have one of those." He made a thought-provoking expression, as if he were delving into his own lost mind. "That's still what I prefer."

"Then there you go. Some things don't change." The dragon lady looked at Allie. "Would you like a drink, too?"

"I think I'll pass."

"Afraid I'll poison it?"

Allie coined Daniel from earlier. "It seems like a possibility."

Glynis rolled her elegantly lined eyes and proceeded to fix the cocktails. For herself, she used a recipe that consisted of vodka, cranberry juice, orange liqueur and fresh lime juice. For Daniel, she poured a jigger of gin over ice and added a twist of lemon peel.

He accepted the drink and made himself at home on the sofa. Allie figured he had a plan, but she wasn't sure what it was. He patted the spot next to him, silently telling her to join him. She did, even if she wasn't comfortable staying any longer than necessary.

Glynis sat across from them and sipped her Vampire's Kiss. Ignoring Allie, she gazed at Daniel. "I can't get over how different you look. How different you seem."

The ice in his glass clinked, and he spoke above

the Gin and Nothing sound. "Do you like me better this way?"

She crossed her legs, flashing her sexy high heels at him. "Would it matter if I did?"

He shrugged, then looked closely at her. "I think I do remember something about you."

She squared her shoulders, lifting her bosom a bit higher. "You do?"

"I seem to recall your pretty handwriting." He paused for effect. "Calligraphy."

Aha, Allie thought. Daniel was trying to trap Glynis. They hadn't told her that calligraphy had been used during the vandalism. If she reacted defensively, she would give herself away.

She didn't get defensive. In fact, she stunned them by saying, "No, no, darling. That's Margaret. She's the one with the lovely penmanship."

"Margaret?"

"My housekeeper."

The bulldog who protected Glynis? Could she be the vandal? Had she done it for Glynis? Were they in on it together? And if they were, why was Glynis being so open about it?

Allie shot Daniel a quick glance. He seemed to be pondering the same questions.

Glynis popped up and walked over to an antique desk and opened the roll top. She returned with a fancy envelope. "Margaret is going to address these for me and mail them later today. See? She already put my return address in her calligraphy."

Daniel took the sealed envelope. "What is this?"

"An invitation. I'm having a Christmas party. Oh, here's a novel idea. Why don't you come?" She turned to Allie. "You, too. Just think, you can stress all evening about me poisoning you. What fun that will be."

Hardy har har. Glynis had a twisted sense of humor. Under different circumstances, Allie might have learned to like her.

Or not.

"We'll think about it," Allie said, wondering if the party had been arranged for her and Daniel's benefit.

"Don't think too long. You'll need to RSVP."

"We'll let you know." Daniel stood up.

"I do hope you'll attend, darling boy. It was so very nice to see you."

Glynis didn't walk them out and neither did Margaret. Daniel and Allie left on their own, the invitation tucked safely into his pocket.

Daniel opened the truck door for Allie and watched her climb inside the vehicle. They didn't discuss the situation, not until he got behind the wheel and started the engine.

"What do you think?" she asked.

That was a loaded question. His mind was crowded and confused, his thoughts clinging like cobwebs. "About Glynis? About Margaret's calligraphy? About whether or not we should go to the party?"

"All of it. But start with Glynis."

He pulled away from the curb. "I honestly don't

remember her. Nor does she seem like my type." Which made his confusion that much greater.

"You don't think she's attractive?"

"It isn't that." Glynis Mitchell had a great body and fascinating sense of style, but she seemed cold and calculating. Not like Allie. He turned away from the windshield to glance at her. "I prefer softer women."

"Maybe you used to like tough girls. I can be tough sometimes, and you used to like me."

Daniel tried not to smile, to make light of her admission. She seemed to believe that her supposed toughness had drawn him to her. But he doubted that was the case.

She fumbled to explain. "Even Glynis commented on your attraction to me."

He decided not to expound on that attraction, to discuss it beyond a few sentences. "I don't trust Glynis. It was rude the way she flirted with me in front of you. Those poison remarks were deliberately bitchy, too."

"Yes, but they seemed more humorous than threatening. Of course, who knows? I never could figure her out."

"And now we've got Margaret thrown into the mix."

"Yes, ugly old Margaret and her pretty calligraphy. Somehow I can't see her being the vandal, not unless she did it for Glynis."

He stopped at a red light. By now, they were in the middle of some fairly heavy traffic. "I'll have Rex run a background check on Margaret, and I'll give Detective Bell the party invitation, so the police can compare her handwriting to the calligraphy on your wall."

"Good idea. We'll wait to see what they say before we decide if we should attend the party."

"I hope we don't have to even consider it. I hope this case is solved before then."

"Me, too."

But how likely was that? Nothing was ever that easy, at least not for Daniel. Having amnesia was making his life seem like a crap shoot.

His cell phone rang and he answered it, using the hands-free device he kept in his car. "Hello?"

"It's Rex."

Before the other man could proceed, Daniel said, "You've got great timing. We just left Glynis's. It's possible that she's the vandal. Her or her housekeeper."

After they discussed what had happened at Glynis's and Rex agreed that a background on Margaret seemed essential, the P.I. stated his business, the reason he'd called.

"I'd like you to meet me at your dad's house tonight. I already spoke to him, and he revealed something about your past that could be pertinent."

"Why can't you tell me now?"

"I think it's something all of us should discuss together."

"All of us?" Daniel assumed that meant Allie, too. Rex wasn't on speaker, so she couldn't hear everything that was being said, but it was enough to make her curious. He could sense her looking at him.

"Is that okay?" Rex asked.

"It's fine." His stomach went tight. "Will this discussion involve a girl from my past?"

"Yes, it will."

He focused on the road, the tightness getting tighter. He didn't dare glance at Allie. "A dead girl?"

Rex's voice jumped. "How did you know that?"

"I just did." Daniel wasn't clairvoyant, but apparently his instincts were strong. "I was having sad feelings about her earlier."

"Do you remember her?"

"No. Just the sadness. Is there a connection between her and the vandal?"

"I can't say for sure, but there could be."

It must be complicated, Daniel thought. If it wasn't, Rex wouldn't have requested a face-to-face meeting. "What time do you want us to meet you?"

"Around seven. Your dad offered to feed us."

Daniel frowned. His old man would probably put on a pot of spaghetti and make a batch of cheese-loaded garlic bread. He would probably try to keep things homey. But maybe that would be less stressful for Allie. She liked gathering around a table. She liked the domestic stuff.

Daniel ended the call, and as soon as he hung up, he waited for her to comment on what she'd heard. She did, after about two beats of heart-thumping silence.

"Rex wants to talk to us about the dead girl," she said.

He nodded. "Strange, isn't it?" Daniel couldn't decide if Rex's timing was coincidence or fate.

"I hope this isn't going to get creepy."

"Me, too," he responded, even though they both knew it was too late for that. It had proved creepy from the start, and it seemed to be getting worse.

Chapter 4

At precisely 7:00 p.m., Daniel escorted Allie into his dad's house. She'd been here a few times before, and she always felt welcome.

Ernie Deer Runner came forward to greet her. Daniel's dad was a tall, slightly paunchy man with a kind and gentle nature.

"How's my girl?" he asked Allie, a smile broadening his face.

"I'm fine."

She leaned in for a hug. She'd first met Ernie when Daniel had been in the coma. He'd asked the ICU staff to allow her to visit his son, even though ICU visitation was normally restricted to immediate family. He'd believed that Daniel would "sense" that Allie was there, and her presence would aid in his recovery.

Allie had believed that, too, especially when Daniel had finally opened his eyes.

But then he'd looked at her with a confused expression, and she'd known instantly that Daniel hadn't recovered, at least not in a way that made it easy for them to resume their lives, to pick up where they'd left off.

Daniel sniffed the tomato and basil in the air and said to his dad, "I knew you'd make a pot of spaghetti."

"It's lasagna, son. I've got a big pan of it in the oven."

"Whatever it is, I'll bet it's going to be good."

"Always." Ernie grinned. "You used to be pretty handy in the kitchen, too. The Deer Runner men have always been the chefs in the family."

"I cooked?"

"I taught you everything I knew."

Daniel glanced at Allie, and they exchanged an amused look. He could barely boil an egg now. But the humor in his eyes died quickly, and Allie suspected that hearing about his old self made him feel like a stranger in his own skin.

"I didn't know you used to cook, either," she said, offering what she hoped was comfort. "You never fixed anything for me. Of course we were too busy fighting witchcraft crimes to do much of anything else." A strange time for all of them, she thought. She'd been cohabitating with Raven and hadn't realized that she loved Daniel until he'd been shot, and the possibility of losing him became a reality.

"And now you have a new crime to fight," Ernie put in.

"So it seems," Allie responded. Daniel was still being quiet.

Was he wondering about his past relationship with her? The things they'd never done? Never shared? Or was he thinking about the purpose of this meeting? The dead girl from his past?

Daniel glanced at his watch. "Rex is late."

"I'm sure he'll be here soon." Ernie gestured to the kitchen, where a Formica table with chrome detail and red vinyl chairs made a vintage statement. "Have a seat, and I'll pour some wine."

"I don't want a drink, Dad."

"I do," Allie piped up. Anything to take the edge off. She made a beeline for the fifties-style kitchen and a sullen Daniel followed.

Ernie seemed happy to play the host. But Allie knew that he liked to keep busy. He also liked to keep things simple and having an amnesiac son appeared to be taking its toll on him.

The older Deer Runner poured two glasses of Chianti, one for Allie and another for himself. He clanked her glass and flashed a troubled smile. "Here's to catching bad guys. Or girls or whichever."

"That works for me." She took a sip.

Daniel kept glancing at his watch, obviously annoyed that Rex still hadn't arrived.

Ernie set a plate of biscotti on the table, offering Allie a nutty-flavored treat before the meal. She went ahead and indulged.

"Dip the cookie in the wine," Ernie coaxed. "I heard that's what they do in Italy."

She tried it. "It's good."

Daniel shook his head. "What are you trying to do, Dad, turn an Indian girl into an Italian? Look at her with all of that blue bling."

"Cut it out." Allie swatted his shoulder. Blue bling was slang for turquoise jewelry. "Stop talking like a rez boy."

He shrugged, and they exchanged conspiratorial smiles. They'd both been born and raised in Los Angeles. She was a city-slick Native, and so was Daniel—even if he barely remembered his upbringing.

Ernie relaxed, too, grateful, it seemed, that his son's mood had improved.

Then the doorbell rang, and everyone tensed all over again.

Daniel stood up. "I'll get it."

He probably wanted to ream Rex for being late, Allie thought. Or maybe he just couldn't stand to sit there and wait for the P.I. to glide onto the scene whenever he so pleased. Rex possessed a nonchalant air. Allie assumed it was the playboy side of him. He was quite obviously a ladies man, a guy who took his God-given charm in stride.

While Daniel went to the door, Ernie checked on the meal. As he prepared a pan of garlic bread to go with the main entree, Allie popped up to help. She couldn't seem to sit still, either.

Soon Daniel returned with Rex. The handsome Sixkiller shook Ernie's hand and gave Allie a quick kiss on the cheek, drawing a scowl from Daniel.

By the time they sat down to eat and discuss the business of the dead girl, Allie's pulse ricocheted. Now she was nervous about Daniel's past, too.

To keep calm, she sipped a second glass of Chianti and complimented Ernie on the food. He'd made marinara sauce for the lasagna, creating a vegetarian dish for her, but he'd also cooked fennel-seasoned sausage for the meat eaters.

Rex started the conversation, speaking directly to Daniel. "The girl was someone you were affiliated with during your senior year of high school. Her name was Susan Delgado. You were with her when she died, along with a group of other kids. You were all swimming in the L.A. River and the current pulled her under. Several of you tried to save her, but…"

Daniel made a pained face and looked to his father for the rest of the story. "Did I ever date her? Was she ever my girlfriend?"

"Not that I know of. But her drowning affected you something fierce. I think she's the reason you enlisted in the army and set about saving the world, so to speak. You weren't much of a fighter before then, but you turned into a warrior after she died."

Allie sat quietly, toying with her food. At this

point, she didn't know what to think, what to feel, except a deep pit of sadness. She could tell that Daniel had more questions.

"Did she drown near Christmastime?" he asked.

Ernie nodded. "It had been a rainy season that year. The water was dirty, as it normally is, and the current was strong. There were signs. No Wading. No Swimming. But you know how teenagers are. You dared each other to jump in anyway."

"I should have saved her." Daniel pushed away his plate. "I was—"

"What?" Rex pressed. "You were what?"

"The best swimmer of all of us," Daniel said. "I was, wasn't I, Dad?"

"Yes. But don't start blaming yourself all over again, son. You did enough of that when it happened."

"Did she have long dark hair?" he asked. "Like Allie's?"

Ernie scooted to the edge of his chair. "Yes, she did. She was about the same height, too. And she had the same slim build. I never really thought about it, but I suppose if you look deep enough, there could be a resemblance." The older man watched his son. "Are you starting to remember her?"

"Maybe. I don't know." Daniel gazed at Allie, and a pin could have dropped. Or a fork or a spoon, she thought. He bumped the table, and she nearly knocked her silverware onto the floor, catching it before it fell.

"Sorry," he said.

"It's okay," she responded, as they stared at each other for a drawn-out moment. Was he looking at her and trying to see Susan?

Finally he broke eye contact and turned to Rex. "Why do you think this could be related to the vandalism?"

"Because Susan has a younger sister, and when you were in the hospital, she sent a get well card. Your dad was surprised to hear from her, but he sent her a thank you note in return. From what he recalls, she blamed you for Susan's drowning. You and all of the other kids who were there."

Daniel blew out a breath. "What's her name?"

"Linda. I ran a quick background on her. She's divorced with a couple of little kids, and she seems normal enough, but that bit about blaming you makes me suspicious."

Daniel squinted at the plate of food he'd pushed away. Allie quit eating and so did Ernie, but Rex maintained an appetite. He poured sauce over bite-size pieces of sausage and added it to his lasagna.

Finally Daniel said, "Maybe when Linda discovered I was in the hospital, it triggered the past and she got remorseful. But maybe later, when she learned how I became injured, she shifted the blame onto Allie. A girl with a resemblance to her sister, a girl I saved instead of her sister. Maybe that's what 'this is for Daniel' meant."

Rex responded, "That's as good a theory as any. I'll give you Linda's contact information so you can pay her a visit. That's what you plan to do, isn't it? Go see her?"

"Absolutely."

Daniel glanced at Allie, and her heart skipped a beat. Now he seemed more protective than ever. He even reached for her hand beneath the table and held it as if he never intended to let go.

When Daniel realized what he'd done, he snapped to attention and released Allie's hand. What was he thinking? Grabbing on to her?

Somewhere in the back of his befuddled mind, he was comparing her to Susan, to a girl he was struggling to remember. Or at least remember in some sort of detail. All he knew was what he felt: a sense of guilt, a sense of grief, a sense of…

Panic.

Of…

Reaching for Susan's hand.

Oh, God, he thought. He did remember. Not enough to recall it clearly, but enough to know that he'd gotten close to saving Susan, until the current had dragged her away from him.

He hoped that Susan's sister wasn't the vandal. He didn't want Allie's torment to be related to Susan's drowning. It was bad enough that he was comparing Allie to the dead girl.

"Was Susan Native?" he asked suddenly.

His dad answered. "Yes, from a California tribe."

Had Susan's heritage made him feel even more responsible for her? Was that part of what had prompted him to become a warrior? To fight for Indian causes?

He questioned his dad again. "Are there any old pictures of her around?"

"I imagine there's one in your senior yearbook. But for the life of me, I don't know where any of that stuff is right now. In the attic, maybe."

"It doesn't matter. I was just curious."

The conversation lulled and dinner ended. Rex thanked his host for the meal, bid everyone goodbye and jetted out the door, probably to meet some hot blonde in a bar.

Allie offered to do the dishes, but Papa Ernie wouldn't hear of it. He shooed her onto the front porch instead, insisting that Daniel join her, and brought them both bowls of ice cream.

Daniel felt as if he were a teenager all over again. Clearly his old man wanted him to hook up with Allie. But the Rocky Road made his dad's interference seem innocent somehow. They sat side by side in wicker chairs.

"This is a nice house," she commented. "It's warm and homey."

"It seems to be." The modest dwelling had been painted a mint shade of green, and wooden white banisters complemented the porch. "But my memories of living here are sketchy."

She looked out onto the grass. "I like the way

your dad decorated the yard. I noticed how cute it was when we first got here."

Christmas crap, Daniel thought. An inflatable Santa sat up high atop a reindeer-driven sleigh, and a slew of animated elves were scattered about like cheap lawn art. Shrubs twinkled with multicolored lights, and big plastic candy canes lined the walkway. "It seems kind of corny to me."

She spooned into her ice cream. "You don't like this time of year, do you?"

"No, I can't say that I do."

"I'll bet it's because Susan drowned near the holidays."

"That's what I was thinking." Up until tonight, he hadn't understood how significant his holiday sadness was. "Dad should have told me about her before now."

"Maybe he didn't want to upset you. Your mind is still fragile."

He frowned at her. He didn't like being called fragile—in any shape or form. "I was only in a coma for a few days. My recovery hasn't been that difficult. I'm well enough to handle this thing with Susan."

"Then you should stop brooding over Christmas and get a tree at your house."

"I will." He tasted his dessert, and the chocolate was cool upon his tongue. He wondered if Rocky Road had been his favorite ice cream when he was a kid. "I'm not that much of a Scrooge. But I'm not putting goofy things in my yard, either."

She shot him a sly smile. "You will if I have anything to do with it."

He smiled, too. He figured it was better than sparring with her. "Yeah, well, you won't. I'm not getting conned by a pretty girl."

"A Christmas con. I like that."

"You would." They laughed, and it felt good to play, to flirt, to be this close to her. But his merriment ended when a tight, secretive feeling came over him.

Secretive how? He honestly didn't know, and that made the feeling worse.

"What's wrong?" she asked, noticing his mood swing.

"Nothing." Except that he hated not remembering his own life. He'd lied about his recovery. It *was* difficult.

"Maybe we should go home."

Home? She made it sound as if they lived together. Well, hell, he thought. They did, at least for now.

As a strand of hair blew across her shoulder and feathered down her arm, he reached out to touch it. Allie's hair. Susan's hair. It tickled his fingers before it left him feeling tight and secretive again.

"I don't want to go home. Not yet." He needed to sit here and try to catch his breath.

"Okay," she said, and focused on her Rocky Road.

As always, she indulged his dark mood. But she'd probably gotten used to the cloudy man he'd become. Versus what? The nerd he used to be? Daniel had seen old photographs of himself and it was tough to relate to the images, especially his superhero glasses.

Fearless Fly indeed. What kind of guy welcomed a nickname like that? A desperate one, no doubt.

When it got too quiet, she said, "It shouldn't be this warm in December. We should be drinking hot chocolate instead of eating ice cream."

"Maybe it will get chillier in the next few weeks." Not that it mattered to him. All he cared about was keeping Allie safe from the person who was using him to get to her. He'd never imagined a scenario like this. He'd never fathomed putting a woman in danger by being the object of another woman's whacked-out obsession.

Or whatever the hell it was.

She clanked her spoon against her bowl. She finished her dessert, as did he, without even realizing it.

"Maybe we should go home now." He wanted to get away from the fat, happy Santa and the motorized elves. Their pointed ears and sparkly green suits were creeping him out, especially now that dusk had turned to night. "Did we ever fight elfish monsters?"

"No. But just about everything in a witchcraft museum came to life."

"As long as it wasn't a Christmas museum. I wouldn't want to have to kick Santa's ass." Or have those little elves gnawing on his flesh.

"Cut it out, Daniel. Quit trying to ruin Christmas."

Was that what he was doing? "Sorry."

She accepted his apology, then stood up and took his empty bowl from him. He followed her into the house and watched the way her body swayed as she walked. She had a natural gait, like a wild creature, he supposed.

Was it any wonder she'd attracted a shape-shifter lover? Daniel didn't remember Raven, but he was able to imagine her in the other man's arms. Most likely, Daniel had been hungry for her when she'd been warming Raven's bed.

It wasn't a comforting thought.

He wanted to pull her tight against him, back to front, like an animal, until he was hard and ready to mate.

That wasn't a comforting thought, either.

They ended the evening with his dad and promised to come back together another time. Much too aware, Papa Ernie watched them leave.

On the way home, Daniel kept quiet. So did Allie. He figured they were both caught up in their own thoughts until they arrived at his house and found a drawing tacked to the front door.

It was a ghoulish rendering of Allie, with cartoonish *X*s over her eyes.

Signaling her death.

Chapter 5

"It's a creative likeness," Allie said, trying to keep herself from getting too fearful. She and Daniel were inside his house now, and Detective Bell had already been called, but how long it would take for him to arrive was anyone's guess. So far, the waiting seemed like forever.

Daniel disagreed with her assessment. "It's cruel and insane."

She rationalized. "The person who drew it is cruel and insane. But the drawing itself has merit."

"So you're saying that your stalker is a fairly decent artist?"

Her stalker. The title was official now. "Yes. It's

patterned after a horror comic. That's the style of art that inspired it."

"Do you know if Glynis has any artistic ability?"

"No, but I suspect that she does." The dragon lady was a walking, talking graphic novel. "If not her, then maybe Margaret. We already established that they could be in this together."

He pondered the other suspect. "I wonder if Susan's little sister likes to draw."

"I don't know, but we're going to have to find out." She plopped down on the sofa and glanced at the sketch again, where it had been placed on the coffee table.

"We should set up a security system with a camera," he said. "In case she comes back. Then we'll have an image of her. Then we'll know who she is."

"That's a good idea."

He sat next to her and patted her knee, rustling the hem of her dress. "Can I get you anything?"

You could kiss me, she thought. "No. I'm okay."

"Are you sure? You're a little pale."

"I'm sure."

They stayed that way for a while, with his hand on her knee, until he seemed to become aware that he was touching her bare flesh. He lifted his hand. "Maybe I should get us both some water."

To quench the heat? To douse their attraction? Somehow she doubted that was going to work. But she said, "I am starting to get thirsty."

"Yeah. Me, too."

He headed toward the kitchen, and she studied the strong, masculine angles of his body, the way his shoulders flared and his hips narrowed. Why did wanting him have to be so complicated?

Because she loved him, her mind answered. But being in love didn't mirror her favorite fairy tale. In the Disney version, Prince Charming didn't have retrograde amnesia, and Cinderella wasn't being stalked by a psycho bitch who wanted her dead.

Daniel returned with two frosty glasses of ice water. He drank his and watched her sip from hers. As the water wet her lips, she battled what she'd been battling all day: the desire to kiss him.

"Are you scared?" he asked.

"Yes." But not just of the stalker. She was afraid of the constant hunger, too.

"I'll keep you safe, Allie. I swear I will."

"I know. I trust you."

"If you have trouble sleeping tonight, you can come to my room."

The glass almost slipped from her hand. Before it hit the carpet and spilled all over the floor, she put it on an end table. "You're inviting me to sleep with you?"

"Not with me. Beside me. We won't do anything."

"We won't?" This was the strangest conversation she'd ever had.

"No. I mean, we can control our urges." He searched her expression. "Right?"

Did he need to prove that they could keep their relationship at a no-sex level, even if they shared the same bed? Was that why he'd made the offer? Or was he truly worried about her being alone, steeped in stalker nightmares? She suspected it was a combination of both.

"Yes," she finally responded. "We can control our urges." They already were, weren't they? By talking about it? By admitting that those types of feelings existed? "But I should be okay tonight." Or so she hoped. "I should just stay by myself."

He sat beside her again. "Is it different this time? Not having it connected to magic?"

"I think it's actually scarier. At least when it was witchcraft, I knew who was behind it. I knew it was my family, my ancestors. I knew who and what I was fighting."

"We'll figure this out. We'll solve it." He frowned at the sketch. "Are you sure you don't want to stay with me tonight?" He lifted his gaze and made eye contact. "I'd feel better having you with me. I could..." He let his words drift.

"You could what?" she asked, pressing an issue that was better left alone.

He blew out an audible breath. "Hold you while you sleep."

She clutched the arm of the couch. "What if you fall asleep first?"

"Fat chance of that. I'm an insomniac, remember?"

Yeah, and a sexy one besides. When he flashed a slight smile, the almost-there curve of his lips made him look like a modern-day rogue.

Her heartbeat accelerated. "Maybe I'll stay with you. I don't know. We'll see." She wanted to, heaven knew she did, but she was already overly attached to him. "I'm trying to be brave on my own."

"I understand." His smile vanished, replaced with an intense look. "Just as long as you know I'm here if you need me."

If only that included needing him for love.

When the doorbell chimed, they both jumped up, assuming it was Detective Bell.

And it was. But his focus-on-the-case presence didn't curb their emotions. He simply took a report and gathered the evidence, leaving them even more aware of each other after he was gone.

Later that night, Daniel tossed and turned. Flailing around in bed was nothing new to him, except for the anticipation of Allie, of wishing she would come to him.

It was masochistic to want her sleeping beside him, but he couldn't help it. He couldn't stand the thought of her being alone with her fears, and he couldn't stand being alone with his.

His what? Fears? Or desires?

Both. The fear of keeping her safe weighed on his mind, right along with heaviness of wanting to put his hands all over her.

But if she did come to him, he wouldn't cross any sexual lines. He would only hold her, the way he'd promised.

Anxious, he glanced at the clock. 12:06 a.m. He'd gone to bed almost an hour ago. Was Allie asleep yet? Or was she tossing and turning, too? He was tempted to get up and go to her room, but that hadn't been the deal. He'd invited her to come to him. The choice was supposed to be based on her needs, on her fears, not on his.

He glanced at the clock again. When it changed to 12:07, he expelled a rough breath. The waiting was killing him.

At 12:18, he heard footsteps in the hallway. His heart struck his chest, especially when his doorknob turned and the door creaked open.

He should have left a light on, but he hadn't wanted to seem too obvious. Now Allie was stumbling around in the dark.

"Daniel?" she said, a question in his name.

"I'm awake." He ignited the bedside lamp, keeping the three-way switch on low and creating a soft glow. He also sat up and looked at her.

Her hair was long and loose, and she wore cotton pajamas with little yellow flowers on them. He wondered if she'd chosen modest bedclothes for his benefit. Last time he'd scolded her for coming to him in a silky nightgown. But this time, he'd invited her. He didn't care if she was sultry or sedate. He desperately wanted her there.

She clasped her hands in front of her, locking her fingers, then unlocking them. She seemed insecure about venturing into his domain. He hoped that she didn't change her mind and bolt out of his room before he got a chance to hold her.

"Close the door," he said, trying to stop that from happening.

She did as she was told, then resumed the same glued-to-the-carpet spot.

He made room for her, scooting closer to the wall.

She finally got into bed, and his hunger for her went haywire. He could smell her shampoo or body lotion or whatever it was, and the floral aroma created a midnight garden.

Now he wanted to inhale her straight into his pores. Lust raged through his blood and tented his pajama bottoms. He almost grimaced from the rising discomfort.

"Will you leave the light on for a while?" she asked.

"Sure." He partially covered her with a blanket. He kept his nether regions covered, too, hiding his desire. They lay side by side, facing each other.

"I wasn't sure if I should do this," she said. "But when I was alone and I closed my eyes, I kept seeing that stupid drawing. It was like seeing myself in a coffin." She sucked nervously on her bottom lip. "So I came to you to make it go away."

And here he was with a hard-on. Talk about wanting something to go away. "I'm sorry."

She blinked at him. "For what?"

"All I can think about is how good you smell."

Her eyes went big and wide. "You're hot and bothered?"

Guilt pummeled him into being honest. "Totally."

"*Daniel.*" She shoved against his bare chest, pushing him away from her, and they both sputtered into anxious laughter.

"I'm sorry," he said again.

"It's okay. Besides, the diversion helps. I'd rather think about you being turned on instead of me being shut in a wooden box." Although she was being flip, she still seemed nervous.

"No one is going to shut you in a wooden box." He wanted to close the gap between them, but he didn't trust himself not to kiss her. "They'd have to put me in one first."

"That almost happened." She glanced at the scar on his chest. Her mood had gone serious. "You almost died for me."

He reduced his heroics to an old adage. "Almost only counts in horseshoes and hand grenades."

"It counted to me."

When she scooted closer, he had to remind himself to breathe. He could tell that she was going to touch his scar.

There it went. Her hand on his skin. He shivered all the way to his toes.

"I was turned on in the truck," she said. "When I was fussing with my seatbelt. That's what was wrong with me."

He hoped this conversation was helping her; it sure as hell wasn't helping him. "But you're not feeling that way now?"

"I'm trying not to. Sex won't solve anything."

Solve, no. Sate, yes. Still, he agreed that it shouldn't happen. Making love would complicate their relationship. They were already closer than they should be, especially for a man with a scattered mind. "We both know better."

"Yes, we do." She removed her hand from his skin. His burning-hot flesh. "I've never done this before."

He fought another shiver. He missed her touch. "Done what? Bunked down with someone who wasn't your lover?"

She nodded. "It's a strange feeling."

For him, too. "I doubt I've done it before, either. Of course I can't remember, so who knows?" Maybe he'd gotten into the habit of torturing himself.

She met his troubled gaze. "Will you hold me now? I want to try to sleep."

"Of course I will." He would deny her nothing, least of all feeling safe in his arms. "But you should turn around so we can do the spooning thing."

"Okay." She rolled over, stirring the mattress and presenting him with a curtain of long dark hair.

He shut out the light, and in the darkness, he pressed against her, curling his body next to hers. If she felt his arousal between them, she didn't comment. She simply let him stay that way.

Hard and hungry and dangerously protective.

Allie awakened in Daniel's arms, all too aware of his body heat, of his fly against her rear. He was still hard. But he couldn't have been that way all night. Could he? Biologically, that didn't seem possible.

No, of course not. He probably had a case of morning wood. An involuntary reaction that occurred during sleep.

She wiggled her butt, and he groaned.

Yikes. He was awake.

"Sorry," she said.

"That's okay." He sounded groggy.

"Did you sleep all right?"

"For a little while. Mostly I just held you."

Before she sighed like a lovesick fool, she sat up to stretch. She'd slept like a baby. No nightmares. No Allie-in-a-box dreams.

He sat up, too. And damn, if he didn't look good. Insomnia worked on him. But everything worked on Daniel. Glasses. No glasses. Slicked hair. Wild, tousled hair. Pajamas. No pajamas.

Not that she'd seen him without, but she could imagine.

She'd behaved herself last night, but her appetite was in full force today. Maybe she should just kiss him and get it over with.

And maybe she should stop craving what she wasn't allowed to have. They'd agreed not to jump each other's bones, and it was a rule they shouldn't break.

"Will you make some coffee?" he asked.

"Sure. You take it black?" She knew he did, but it gave her something to say.

"The stronger the better. Just call me when it's ready."

"That's all right. I'll bring it in here." Like a lover, she thought. Or a girlfriend. Or a wife.

She darted out the door and down the hall to brew the coffee. When she returned, two cups in hand, Daniel was waiting for her.

"Thanks." He took the offering.

"You're welcome."

Their gazes met over the rims of their cups, and she longed to curl back up in his arms. The more time she spent with Daniel, the harder she fell.

"We probably shouldn't do this again," she said.

"Have coffee?"

She lifted her brows. He knew darn well what she meant. "Sleep together, smarty."

"Nothing happened."

"We wanted it to."

"Yeah, but it didn't."

"And that makes it okay?" He shouldn't have invited her to his room last night, and she shouldn't have remained in bed with him this morning. Coffee or not.

Flustered, she set her cup on the nightstand.

He discarded his cup, too. Then he poked at her ribs, tickling her, teasing her, trying to lighten her mood.

She batted his hand away. "Cut it out."

He tickled her again, and she managed to laugh, to give into his playfulness. Nonetheless, she was hurting inside. Longing for love and getting a crazy, mixed-up flirtation in return.

"Do you even remember what sex is like?" she asked.

He stopped goofing around. "Sort of."

"Sort of?" she parroted.

"I remember how good it feels, but I don't remember engaging in the act itself, of being with anyone. I have a lot of those kinds of memories. Feelings. Not images."

"Are you going to be nervous the first time it happens?"

"Why would I be? It won't be my *real* first time."

"I know, but…"

"Don't worry about me. I'll figure things out."

Yes, she imagined that he would. But with whom? If she didn't make love with him, then who would be his partner? The thought of him dating someone else made her heart go unbearably tight.

"I think you should wait," she said.

"For what?"

"Nothing. I don't know." She glanced away, struggling for a change of topic.

He glanced away, too, and they both zeroed in on the clock. It was almost nine.

"When are we going to see Susan's sister?" she asked, grateful that she'd thought of something legitimate to say.

"As soon as I give her a call. Rex said she runs a computer business from home."

"So we're going over there today?"

He nodded. "I keep wondering if there was something more between Susan and me."

"More than friendship? Your dad said there wasn't."

"I know. But what if there was?"

Allie hoped there wasn't. She'd been through something similar with Raven, and she didn't want to go through it with Daniel, too. She couldn't bear for him to be hung up on a girl from his past.

Living or dead.

Chapter 6

Linda Delgado-Forster lived in a noisy neighborhood, in a house surrounded by a chain-link fence and a big, overgrown yard. Toys and bikes littered the driveway and a yappy dog, a shaggy terrier of some kind, pretended to patrol the grounds.

Allie and Daniel opened the gate and entered the property and the pooch quit barking and ran to greet them. Daniel reached down to pet him. So did Allie. He was a cute little guy.

Was his mistress a crazy stalker? Or was she just a hard-working single mom being wrongly suspected? Allie didn't have a clue, and she doubted that Daniel did, either. He'd called ahead to let Linda know he would be stopping by with a friend named

Allie, and she'd seemed surprised to hear from him. She also reacted, at least on the phone, as if she didn't know who Allie was. Would she be as convincing in person?

A ring of the doorbell would soon tell. Or maybe not. The bell didn't work. Daniel knocked instead, and Allie glanced his way.

"On the day I first came to your house, your doorbell was broken, too," she said. "Your place was rundown then. You were still in the process of fixing it up."

"I think you told me this before."

"Did I?" She was always repeating stories from the past, hoping to trigger his memory, if that was even possible. "A mutual friend from the Warrior Society put me in touch with you. I came there to ask you about ravens." Not only because he was a veterinary technician and had knowledge of birds, but because he was affiliated with the Haida Nation, and Raven was a demigod in that culture. Not Allie's Raven. He was a real man who'd been cursed by witchcraft. The Haida Raven was a mythological creature.

Daniel knocked on the door again.

"Your mother was from the Raven Clan," she said.

"I know."

"Is that something you remember? Or something I already told you?"

"I remember," he responded, then added, "*Hoya,*" using the Native word for his mother's clan.

The dog at their feet wiggled and danced, waiting for the door to open. Allie and Daniel waited, too.

"I wonder if Linda decided to avoid us," she said.

He knocked louder.

Finally the door flew open, and there stood a full-figured woman with medium-length, straight brown hair and no makeup. Two little girls appeared beside her. They wore matching play clothes and curious expressions. They appeared to be around six and seven. Allie assumed they weren't in school because they were on Christmas break.

"Daniel?" the mom at the door said. The dog ran past her and went into the house.

"Yes."

"You look different from the boy I remember. But life changes us, doesn't it?" She turned to Allie. "You must be the friend he mentioned. I'm sorry I didn't answer right away, but I didn't expect you so soon. I was helping the girls with their bath."

The children grinned, and they were as cute as could be. Allie hoped Linda wasn't the stalker. She certainly didn't seem like a whacko. She was well spoken and personable. But that didn't mean that she didn't have a warped mind.

"Come in," she said, and gently nudged her kids to make room for them.

Daniel smiled at the little girls, and Allie's heart went pitter-pat. She hoped Linda's heart wasn't pitter-pattering, too. The other woman started fussing with her appearance, smoothing her hair and tugging at her clothes, as if she wished she'd taken the time to fix herself up a bit. Instead, she'd gotten her kids ready. They each had pretty barrettes in their freshly washed hair.

Linda offered her guests a seat in her living room. It wasn't spick-and-span clean, but it wasn't as cluttered as the front yard, either. Apparently the kids weren't allowed to leave toys lying around the house.

She sent the girls to their room so the grown-ups could talk. Once the kids were gone, she said to Daniel and Allie, "I can put on a pot of tea if you'd like."

They declined, and for a moment, everyone was silent. Then Daniel said, "Thanks for seeing us."

He and Allie had discussed their approach ahead of time and had agreed that they wouldn't come right out and accuse Linda the way they'd done with Glynis. They would use a less invasive method.

"I don't understand why you're here," Linda said. "You didn't explain yourself clearly on the phone."

He responded, "I wanted to thank you in person for the get well card you sent when I was in the hospital."

"Oh, that." Linda made an open gesture. "I felt badly for what happened to you. I read about it in the paper. You thwarted a robbery at a museum and got shot."

Allie shifted in her chair. She and Daniel had actually been part of the robbery. They'd broken into the witchcraft museum that housed a talisman that could set Raven free, intending to steal it. But another thief, a dangerous witch, was already there, waiting for them. After the shooting, the museum director concocted a story that had absolved Daniel and Allie from any wrongdoing, and that was the version that had been fed to the press.

"I didn't know you'd sent a card," Daniel said. "My dad hadn't told me about it until yesterday."

"That's okay. I imagine you've had a lot going on with your recovery." Linda gave him a faint smile. "You look well now."

"Except for my mind."

Her smile vanished. "What do you mean?"

"I have amnesia. Didn't you know?"

"Oh, my. No." Her reaction seemed genuine, but maybe she was a good actress. "Is it because of the coma you were in?"

"Yes." He offered more information. "I don't remember you, but I recall snippets about Susan."

At the mention of her sister's name, Linda's eyes clouded. She blinked and blew out a sigh. "I named my oldest daughter after her." She kept talking, confiding in Daniel. "I still miss Susan, but I quit blaming you and the other kids a long time ago. She jumped into the river on her own. No one forced her to do it."

He cleared his throat. "I tried to save her."

"I know." She expelled another sigh. "That's why I quit blaming everyone. You all tried to save her." She shifted her attention to Allie. "Did you know my sister?"

"No. I'm sorry, I didn't."

"You actually look a bit like her. Don't you think so, Daniel?"

"My dad said that, too. But I can't remember what Susan looked like."

"Oh, goodness. Really?" The other woman scooted forward. "I have a picture in the den. Hold on."

She left and came back with a framed photograph. She handed it to Daniel.

He stared at it for what seemed like forever. When he glanced up, Linda was watching him. So was Allie.

Daniel asked Linda, "Do you know if your sister was seeing anyone? Or if there was a boy she liked?"

"She was supposed to go to the prom with Todd Monroe."

"Was he there the day of the drowning?"

"No, he wasn't. I guess it's safe to assume that you don't remember him." She shook her head. "Having amnesia must be awful."

"Was Susan ever involved with me?" he asked.

Linda said, "Not that I'm aware of."

She'd given the same response as Daniel's father, Allie thought. As far as anyone knew, Susan and Daniel hadn't been an item.

Nonetheless, Allie noticed discomfort in Daniel's eyes. Was he still debating if he and the dead girl had harbored feelings for each other?

He took one last look at Susan's picture. Then he passed it to Allie.

She studied the image of a teenager with long hair, tanned skin and a breezy smile. It was strange to search for herself in someone so young, but a haunting resemblance was there. Mostly it was the hair, although they had similar bone structure, too.

Everyone appeared to be waiting for her to comment, but she didn't know what to say.

Finally she spoke, giving Susan life beyond the grave. "I wonder if she would have grown up to look like me."

Linda took the picture. "It's hard to say. She might have gained weight the way I have. I used to be skinny, too, before I started eating so much to fill the void."

"Of losing your sister?" Allie asked.

"Of going through an emotional break-up."

Linda didn't seem like a stalker. If anything, she seemed like a typical divorcee, struggling to get her life back on track.

But Daniel wasn't ready to throw in the towel. He asked her, "Was Susan good at art?"

"No. Why?"

"It's just something I thought I remembered." He segued into Linda's artistic abilities, the true reason he'd brought up the subject. "What about you? Do you draw or paint?"

If the question alarmed her, she didn't let it show; she didn't react as if she'd left a gruesome drawing on his door the night before. She laughed and said, "Not unless coloring with my daughters could be considered art."

Her genuine nature made it tough to keep suspecting her.

But still...

After Daniel and Allie left, he said, "I don't think it's her. But we're not ruling her out. Not completely."

Because anything was possible, Allie thought. Anyone was capable of being secretly insane.

Two days went by and nothing happened. No vandalism. No death threats. No more clues. Then the phone rang in the middle of the afternoon, and Daniel answered it.

Detective Bell was on the other line with information about the handwriting analysis. Daniel listened to what the cop had to say and frowned at the receiver.

"I'll tell Allie," he said, and thanked the detective for his time. Time was all they seemed to have. Too much of it.

Daniel peeked into the third bedroom, which Allie had set up as a makeshift studio. She stood in front of an easel, creating a light-hearted watercolor: a wood nymph with butterfly wings.

"Hey," he said, by way of capturing her attention.

She turned around, and they gazed at each other. In the nights that passed, she hadn't come back to his bed, but he hadn't expected her to. Regardless, he missed holding her, waking up next to her, keeping her as close as he possibly could.

He explained the interruption. "Detective Bell called. They can't tell if the party invitation envelope and the message at your loft was written by the same person. According to the analysis, the calligraphy on your wall was scripted with a stencil, and the envelope was done freehand."

"So that's it?" She put down her brush. She had pretty little pastel paint droplets on her top. "We're back to square one."

"At least we have some suspects."

"And they're all shaky, at best. We don't have anything linking them to the original crime scene. Or to the drawing."

"The police are still investigating."

"With what tools? They didn't find any identifiable fingerprints at my loft."

"They collected hair samples."

"They'll probably turn out to be mine. Or yours or Olivia's or West's."

Olivia was Allie's sister, and West was the FBI husband. Daniel didn't remember them from before, but he'd gotten to know them over the past few months. "The lab hasn't gotten the results back, so we'll just have to wait and see."

She made a face. "I hate waiting."

"I know. Me, too. Maybe we should call West and Olivia. It wouldn't hurt to have a psychic and a special agent helping us on the case, and I'm sure they would want to know what's going on."

"I'm not destroying my sister's honeymoon over this. They deserve some time alone."

"Yes, but—"

"But nothing. Do you know how long it took for

West to propose? And for her to accept? They're not exactly the most romantic couple."

All the more reason to intrude on their honeymoon, he thought, to bring them into the fold.

Allie balked. "If you call them, I'll never forgive you."

He considered shaking some sense into her, but he knew how determined she could be. Besides, he didn't want to be on her unforgiven list.

She changed the subject. "I think I should go back to work."

"You are working." He gestured to her painting.

"I was talking about the senior center."

"It's too soon." He couldn't stand the thought of her being away from him, not while the case was pending, not while the stalker was still out there. "We took a vacation from our jobs."

"But I'm going stir-crazy. I can't concentrate." She glanced at her work in progress. "Look at that. It's crap."

He thought the painting was beautiful, but he doubted that his opinion would matter. He wasn't an art connoisseur. "Just wait until your vacation time is over." Then they would both be forced to return to their jobs, to resume their incomes. "By then, we'll catch the stalker and everything will be okay."

"Promise?"

He nodded, even though he shouldn't have. There were no guarantees. "I'll keep you busy until then."

"Doing what?"

He couldn't think of anything, so he said, "Stuff."

She crossed her arms. "What stuff?"

He wracked his brain for a response and came up with, "You can help me get this place ready for Christmas."

"Really?" Her soulful eyes went bright. "Oh, Daniel, that's perfect. It's just what we need to stay occupied."

We? He'd concocted the holiday activity for her, not for himself. But seeing her smile was worth it. He got the urge to scoop her into his arms, but he refrained from making physical contact.

"We'll start with a tree," she said. "Then we'll go from there."

As long as they didn't go too far. He wasn't decorating his front yard. No mistletoe, either. He was having enough don't-kiss-her trouble.

"I'll get ready and we can head out," Allie said.

"Right now?"

"Yes, right now. We need to find the perfect tree."

Which meant what? That it could take all day? He'd more or less planned to grab the first green bush he saw. "How about a fake one?" He'd seen some easy fold-out models at Wal-Mart. No fuss. No muss.

"An artificial tree might work. That way, you'll have it from year to year." Her eyes went bright again. "They have some beauties at the Christmas Store."

"The Christmas Store?" What had he gotten himself into? "Where's that?"

"At the mall. It changes, depending on the time of year. In October, it's the Halloween Store."

"All right. We'll go there." Honestly, he thought. How big could a store like that be? How much junk could they have? A lot, his logical mind said. Christmas galore.

"Do you have any decorations for the tree?"

"I don't know. I suppose I do. Somewhere." Surely he had a box in the garage or the attic or in the storage shed out back.

"Somewhere?" She made disapproving sound. *Tsk-tsk.*

"Hey, I have amnesia. What do you expect?"

"You wouldn't remember where the decorations were even if you didn't have amnesia."

Okay, so she had a point. "I'll buy a few new things."

She clapped her hands together. "This is going to be fun."

Daniel couldn't stop himself from smiling. She was sweeter than a grown woman had the right to be. "I'll bet you shook all of your presents when you were a kid."

"When I was a kid?" She laughed. "I still shake them."

"Do you want to exchange presents this year?" he asked, even though he didn't have a clue what to get her.

"Are you joking? Me? The Christmas con? I'd love to. I already have something special in mind for you."

The sudden tenderness in her eyes had him wondering just how special her gift would be.

"I'll go get ready." She flitted off to change her

clothes and reapply her makeup or whatever it was women did to make themselves more presentable.

He popped open a soda and waited at the kitchen table. He wasn't going to brood. He wasn't going to spoil her Christmas cheer. But that didn't mean that he couldn't contemplate how strange his relationship with Allie was.

They'd agreed to keep things platonic. But their attraction dictated just about every breath they took.

Thirty minutes later, she returned looking sleek and gorgeous. She was dressed all in black, like her cat, except for a chain belt and sterling jewelry.

"Wow." The word almost got trapped in his throat.

She sent him a beguiling smile. "You like what you see?"

"Hell, yeah." Too much, he thought.

She moved forward, and his ever-present hunger reared its desperate head.

He wanted to say, "Screw platonic." But he didn't do it. He didn't take advantage of Allie.

They left the house together, making the most out of being friends.

Or whatever it was they were.

Chapter 7

Upon entering the Christmas Store, Daniel said, "Wow."

The same word he'd used to describe her, Allie thought. She'd taken extra care with her appearance and it paid off. Daniel liked the way she looked. Not that she had any business trying to get his attention. Friends weren't supposed to entice other friends.

But friends with benefits were.

Maybe she could have sex with him and still keep their friend status. Maybe she could talk herself out of being in love with him.

Oh, sure. As if it was that easy. Allie lived by her heart, and she would probably die by it, too.

Die by it? She rubbed a sudden rush of goose bumps on her arms.

"Look how many they have," Daniel said, referring to an impressive display of decorated trees.

She snapped back to holiday mode. "You can have your pick."

"No kidding." He pointed to an artificial Douglas fir decorated with red and gold ornaments. "I wonder if they sell their floor models. We could grab this one and go, with all the trimmings."

"Where's the fun in that?"

He flashed a diabolical grin that made him look like the Grinch. "Who said this was supposed to be fun?"

"Me, you Christmas ogre." She bumped his shoulder, and they laughed. She loved laughing with him. The combined sound was soft yet husky. They melded well together.

"All right," he said. "We can pick out our own trimmings. But I still like that style of tree."

"Sounds good to me."

They went up and down aisles that housed hundreds of traditional ornaments. They browsed unconventional items, too.

"Check this out," she said. "They have wildlife ornaments. You should get these, Daniel." She thought they complemented his style. "You love exotic animals." He also worked with them at his job. "You couldn't ask for a better fit."

"A wildlife tree. That is kind of cool. But we should get something that represents you, too."

"Me?" She got fluttery inside. That happened a lot when she was with him. She behaved like a schoolgirl. When an image of Susan came to mind, she willed it away. Schoolgirl hadn't been a good reference.

"Let's see." He stood back to study her. "What types of ornaments say Allie Whirlwind? Oh, I know. How about the types of things you paint?"

"I'd be a fantasy tree?"

He grinned, but it wasn't a Grinch grin. This time, it was oh, so sexy. "Fantasy is a great way to describe you."

"I wasn't talking about *those* kinds of fantasies." Regardless, she adored the devilishness in his smile, the primal manner in which he flirted.

Friends with benefits, she reminded herself. He would probably jump at the chance if she presented it to him that way.

"How about if we get heart-shaped ornaments?" she said.

"Hearts?" He wrinkled his forehead.

"Sometimes I paint knights in shining armor and damsels in distress."

"I don't want a love tree, Allie."

"That isn't how I meant it." Liar, she thought. Love was always on her mind. "Just think about what's going on. I'm the damsel in distress and you're my knight. The hearts aren't just me. They're us."

"You're too damn girly, you know that? But we'll throw in a heart or two, along with exotic animals and fantasy creatures and whatever else strikes our fancy." He laughed. "This is going to be one weird-ass tree."

She laughed, too, enjoying his colorful description.

They got a cart and filled it with eclectic ornaments, twinkling lights, retro-style tinsel and an enchanted angel for the top. As for the tree itself, he stuck to his original selection: the artificial, six-foot fir.

Once they were home, they dived into their project, and she knew this was going to be her favorite Christmas ever.

Because she was spending the season with him. A season of the heart, she thought. Her heart. Trussed up on a tree and hopelessly in love.

Allie couldn't sleep, but she knew what would happen if she went to Daniel's room. She would give up the fight and make long, hard, emotional love with him. The passionate moment kept getting closer. *They* kept getting closer.

Needing a diversion, she decided to fix a midnight snack.

On the way to the kitchen, she stumbled across Daniel. He sat on the living room floor, staring at the Christmas tree. He must have gotten out of bed and come here, the way a small child would. Only he didn't look like a holiday-eyed kid. He looked like the troubled man he was.

He turned and noticed her, and neither of them spoke. The lights on the tree blinked on and off, twinkling in the semi-darkness.

He checked her out, his gaze sweeping up and down. She didn't know what to do, so she stood like a lingerie-store mannequin and let him devour the nightgown-draped length of her.

Self-conscious as she was, he made her feel like a seductress. All she had to do was reach for his hand and lead him astray. But that would mean leading herself astray, too.

She broke the ice and said, "I was on my way to get a snack." She wanted him to know that her presence in the living room wasn't purposeful. "But maybe I'll stay here with you instead."

"That would be nice. You look really pretty." He turned away from her. "The tree is pretty, too."

Talk about an abrupt transition. Clearly, he was in an odd frame of mind. She took a seat on the couch and waited to see what else he would say.

He continued, "The more I look at it, the more I like it. It's not as weird as I thought it would be."

"I like it, too." But she hadn't gotten out of bed to stare at the tree. Of course, now she was immersed in it, too. "We did good."

"Yeah, we did. It still disturbs me, though."

She knew he meant Christmas. "You're still going to celebrate it, aren't you?" They'd agreed to exchange gifts, but maybe that was as far as he intended to go.

"My dad would pitch a fit if I didn't."

She got a brainstorm. "Do you think we could spend Christmas here?"

"Instead of going to my dad's?"

"I'm sure he would be glad to come here. He could help me with the meal. We could invite a few friends, too."

"I suppose that would be all right. Will Olivia and West be back by then?"

"They'll still be in Europe." Nonetheless, she wanted to entertain with Daniel. She wanted them to seem like a couple.

He stood up, came over to the couch and sat beside her. He was wearing his typical nighttime attire: a pair of low-slung pajama bottoms. She imagined leaning forward to kiss him.

"I've been thinking about Glynis's party," he said.

So much for romance, she thought. Not that she was brave enough to make it happen anyway. "What about her party?"

"We should probably attend. Just to see what unfolds."

"I agree. We should. We can RSVP tomorrow."

They both fell silent, until he glanced up at the angel on the tree. "It isn't the religious part of Christmas that disturbs me."

"I didn't think that it was." She knew he was a devout Catholic. He went to Mass every Sunday. His faith had gotten him through the darkness they'd endured—the bewitched creatures, the tragic ghosts. He'd even brought holy water to the final museum showdown.

"It's all the other stuff," he explained. "The phony cheer."

"It's not phony to everyone. Some people genuinely love it."

"Like you?"

"Yes, like me. You know what else we should do tomorrow?"

"Besides RSVP the party? I don't have a clue."

"We should make rock candy together."

"The hard stuff that melts in your mouth?"

Her pulse jiggered. "Yes." Rock candy had never sounded so sexy.

"Is that one of your usual holiday activities?"

"I make gingerbread houses, too."

He smiled. "Now why doesn't that surprise me?" He quit smiling. "Do you know why I came in here to look at the tree?"

She shook her head.

"I was trying to remember more about Susan. I was trying to feel more connected to her. Since she died during Christmastime, I thought the tree might help."

"Did it?"

"Yes. I've been having this tight, secretive feeling, and tonight I realized it was a memory." He paused, then added, "Susan wasn't my girlfriend, but I was in love with her."

Allie's heart punched her chest. This was exactly what she didn't want to hear. "You were awfully young, Daniel."

"Not too young to fall in love. Or to keep my feelings a secret. I never told her. I just suffered through it."

Talk about suffering. And keeping secrets.

"Not that it matters," he said. "She's been dead a long time, and I'm not ready to fall in love again."

Was that a warning? Did he suspect how Allie felt about him? Or was he trying to talk himself out of feeling too much?

"I understand," she said, even though she didn't understand at all.

In the morning, Allie and Daniel went to the store and got the ingredients for the rock candy, and now they were in the kitchen, preparing to make the holiday treat.

Caught in the throes of last night's conversation, she struggled to concentrate. All she could think about was Daniel not being ready to fall in love again. The more she obsessed about it, the more she feared that he'd never loved her in the past, that Susan had been the only one.

"Red and green." He commented on the food coloring she'd chosen. "Christmas all the way."

She gave him a distracted nod.

"Are you okay, Allie?"

She paused, then said, "I'm fine." She wasn't about to explain her emotions to him.

"No, you're not. I can tell you're preoccupied. But don't worry about the stalker. The case is getting handled. I talked to Rex earlier, and he's been interviewing the other Warrior Society guys about me."

The stalker hadn't been on her mind this morning, but she let him assume that was the cause of her preoccupation. "Has anything turned up that could be helpful?"

"Not yet. No one seems to know much about my personal life. But I'm sure something will surface. I couldn't have been that secretive."

"You were with Susan," she said, before she could stop herself.

"That's different."

Because he'd loved her, Allie thought, the reminder kicking her in the gut.

He jumped back to their original topic. "Rex is going to investigate old Warrior Society cases, too. It's possible that the stalker became associated with me through one of my missions."

"Your specialty was recovering lost and stolen artifacts."

"It still is."

"Yes, of course." His amnesia hadn't affected his ability to serve the Society. Daniel Deer Runner was still a warrior. And a justifiable thief. When all else failed, he stole back objects and returned them to their rightful owners.

He stole hearts, too. Hers was pounding like crazy. "We should get started on the candy."

He glanced at the supplies: glass jars, pencils with strings attached, a thermometer. "Looks like a science experiment."

"It can be." She set two saucepans on the stove. "Pharmacists used to make rock candy as medicine."

"Not for diabetes, I hope." He grinned and reached for the sugar.

She couldn't help but return his goofy smile. She knew he was trying to cheer her up.

Soon they were standing side-by-side at the stove, each stirring a pan of a sugar and water mixture, heating it until the sugar dissolved.

Gradually, they added food coloring. She gave him green and took red for herself.

The blood-colored liquid sent unexpected shivers down her spine.

Apparently the stalker was on her mind this morning. Or at least in her subconscious.

"Am I doing this right?" he asked.

"You're doing fine." She was the one having trouble.

He glanced at her mixture, but he didn't remark that it looked like blood. His imagination probably wasn't as distorted as hers. Either that or he was too focused on his green goop to notice.

"How long does the candy take to crystallize?" he asked.

"It will be edible within an hour. But it's better to let the crystals form for about a week."

"It's quite a process."

She nodded, and they continued working side-by-side. Following the recipe she always used, they poured their solutions into jars.

The red looked just as icky that way.

From there, they placed pencils over the mouth of the jars so crystals could form along the strings.

"That was kind of fun," Daniel said.

"Really?" She relaxed a little. "You liked it?"

"Yeah, I did. Maybe I should experiment with real food, too."

"You want to learn to cook?"

"My dad said I used to be good at it. So maybe it's still inside me. Maybe I just need to spend more time in the kitchen and let it happen."

"You want to go back to being who you were?"

"Not completely. Not the nerd with the glasses."

"I liked him." Loved him, she amended in her mind.

"Why? Because he was a nice guy? You know what they say about nice guys."

"You never finished last."

"Didn't I? Maybe I was secretive about my love life because it sucked."

"And maybe you were just being a gentleman and not talking about it. You know what I used to like? The way your hair smelled."

"Because of the Brylcreem?"

"My dad used to use it, too. It was familiar. Comforting, I guess."

"I don't comfort you now?"

"Of course you do." She reached out to smooth a strand of his naturally messy hair. "The night you held me was one of the most comforting nights of my life."

"Then why haven't you come back to me?"

She dropped her hand. "You know why."

He leaned against the counter, but not in a casual

way. His muscles were taut. "I still find myself waiting up for you."

Her body went deliciously, fearfully warm. Regardless, she tried to make light of a conversation that had gone lust deep. "You'd stay awake, anyway."

"Because I'm an insomniac? It's not same as lying there, hoping you'll come to me."

"We shouldn't be talking about this." Not when she was on the verge of offering herself to him.

He cleared a raspy sound from his throat, a roughness that made him even sexier. "You're right. I'm sorry."

She turned away to free her mind, to get her emotional bearings. But it didn't help. She caught sight of the red jar, inciting the creep factor again.

Nothing was going Allie's way today.

Nothing at all.

Chapter 8

On the night of Glynis's party, Allie wore a new outfit, chosen specifically for the occasion.

She stood in front of the mirror and examined her appearance. Her long, body-clinging dress was crimson silk. Yes, the color of blood. To prove that she wasn't afraid.

The side slits were for Daniel. He was a leg man. Or he had been before the amnesia. She could only hope that he still was.

As for her shoes, they were leopard-print pumps. Again, for Daniel. He was partial to faux fur.

Would Daniel say "wow" when he saw her?

Adding yet another wild dimension, she'd created

a sexy mane out of her hair, pinning part of it up and allowing the rest to fall free.

The final touch was no underwear. No bra. No panties. Her braless look was evident, considering the hardness of her nipples, but no one, besides herself, would know that she was going commando. Still, it made her feel hot and lethal.

Glynis had nothing on her.

Not unless Glynis was the stalker. Allie frowned at her femme fatale reflection. The stalker had been lying low, whoever she was.

Would something threatening happen at this party? Or was getting dolled up and going out with Daniel the only danger?

She checked her makeup one last time. Smoky eyes, glossy lips. Allie was ready to take on the world. All she needed was a pearl-handled Derringer in her purse to complete the picture. But she didn't own a girly gun. What she owned was a Dirty Harry-style .44 Magnum, the very gun her father had used to commit suicide.

Regardless, Allie had forgiven him for his horribly destructive act, especially since she'd communicated with his ghost. When Daniel had been in the hospital, Dad had appeared at his bedside, putting Raven's talisman around his neck. By that time, Raven had already gone to the Apache underworld, sending Allie's dad as his messenger.

Then, just seconds before Daniel had opened his eyes, her father faded away, moving onto the Lakota Ghost Road. The amulet had disappeared, too. Magic that had been powerful enough to release Daniel from a coma, but not strong enough to restore his memories.

Returning to the present and talking to a spirit who was no longer earthbound, she said, "I love him, Dad. I love him so much. But you knew how I felt. That's why you helped him recover."

In the silence, she thought about another dead person. Susan. The girl Daniel claimed to have loved.

"Should I be appealing to you?" Allie asked Susan. "To help Daniel remember his past? To help us catch the stalker? Or is it your sister doing those awful things? We don't think it's her, but we don't know for sure."

Once again, Allie was met with silence. But she didn't expect an apparition. She didn't feel the presence of Susan's ghost.

A knock rattled the door, and her pulse beat against her body. She knew it was Daniel. They were the only people there.

She tugged at the scooped neckline of her dress. Now her nipples were even harder. "Come in."

He entered the room, took one look at her and uttered, "Damn."

"Damn" sounded far more delicious than "wow." He was staring at her as if she were a sweet and creamy dessert.

She stared at him, too. He was dressed in a classic black suit, paired with a trendy shirt. He'd combed his hair straight back. She moved closer to see if he'd used tonic. He had. Not as much as he used to, but she could smell a faint aroma of Brylcreem.

Touched by his sentiment, she said, "A little dab'll do ya," mimicking the old TV ads.

He smiled and ran his hand through his slicked hair, messing it up a little. The result was beyond sexy.

"We're going to be the most dashing couple at the party," she said.

"I don't know about me, but you look amazing, Allie. I couldn't have dreamed a more beautiful girl."

"Thank you." If he knew that she was *completely* naked underneath, he would probably moan on the spot. Already he was sliding his gaze from her braless breasts to the high-cut slits on the sides of her dress. He even glanced at her bed.

Was he picturing her strewn upon it?

"Ready to go?" he asked.

She nodded, mentally preparing herself for whatever the night would bring. She didn't expect Glynis to poison her. The other woman was too shrewd to do anything that obvious. But Allie was uneasy just the same.

Daniel looked into her eyes. Or maybe he was looking into her soul. He noticed her reluctance.

He said, "I'll be by your side the entire time."

Once again, she inhaled the familiar scent of his hair. She desperately wanted to touch it, to touch *him,* but she knew this wasn't the time or place.

They had a holiday gathering to attend, and while they were there, they intended to keep an eye on Glynis and Margaret, along with other guests and anyone else who might be the stalker.

A short time later, they arrived at their destination. Margaret answered the door and gave them the once over.

"We were invited," Daniel said, warning the bulldog not to block their way.

"I'm aware of who's on the guest list. But I don't have to like it," she mumbled loud enough for them to hear.

Old biddy, Allie thought. Tonight she was attired in a maid's uniform, a starched white dress, with a glittering Christmas tree pin attached to her lapel. But it wasn't any old pin; it actually looked like the real deal. Allie suspected that the jewels were genuine. A gift from her eccentric boss? Payment for stalker services rendered?

Margaret granted them entrance and begrudgingly offered to take Allie's wrap. If she was guilty of the crime, she wasn't making any bones about it. Then again, Rex hadn't uncovered anything in her background check that screamed "stalker!"

The party was in full swing, and the house looked spectacular. Daniel and Allie joined the other guests in a garden room filled with festive food and stocked with liquor. Scores of extravagant hors d'oeuvres were presented on a buffet table, and a handsome young man tended bar.

Leaded glass doors led to the backyard, where decorative brickwork and a collection of café tables made a lovely retreat. A stone fire ring created nighttime warmth. The weather had cooled off a bit, and the setting was perfect for a southern California gathering. Beyond the patio was a dazzling garden, with elegant bridges and fish ponds.

Glynis was outdoors, seated at one of the café tables and smoking a cigarette from an art deco holder. Her 1930s-style dress was gold lamé and her emerald necklace appeared to be from the same era. She was chatting amicably with a group of equally glamorous people.

She turned and saw Allie and Daniel. She got up and came toward them, gliding across the patio, cigarette and holder still in hand.

"The dragon lady approaches," Allie said.

"I wonder if she'll blow smoke in our faces," Daniel responded.

She did no such thing. Instead she gave each of them a Hollywood hug, while keeping her cigarette at a proper distance. She smelled like tobacco splashed with Chanel No. 5. Trust Glynis to favor the oldest, most high society signature fragrance of its time.

"Allie," she said, catty as ever. "You look stunning. And you," she roamed her saucy gaze over Daniel, "are almost as yummy as my soon-to-be new boy toy." She gestured to the bartender. "I've got my sights on that one."

"Too bad for him," Allie said.

"Now, don't be bitchy. This is a party after all."

"Sorry." Allie faked an apology. "My manners must have slipped. That happens when one is being stalked."

"I already told you that I wouldn't waste my time with something that petty."

"Petty? You should see the picture my stalker drew. Oh, wait, maybe you already did. Maybe Margaret drew it."

"Margaret? My housekeeper wouldn't draw you a bath, let alone a picture."

"Not even a ghoulish one?"

Glynis raised her brows. "Just how ghoulish was it?"

"Horror comic book style."

"Really? Well, that's hardly Margaret's forte. She paints landscapes."

"So, you're not denying that she's an accomplished artist?" Daniel interjected.

"I wouldn't say that she's accomplished. She merely dabbles." The dragon lady turned to Allie. "You're the professional artist. Oh, here's a thought. Maybe you drew it yourself. Maybe you're doing all of this for attention."

Allie wanted to choke Glynis with her big, sparkling emeralds. "This from the dame of death?"

"I got over that a long time ago. I much prefer the living. Now, let's quit quarreling and relax, shall we? I'll finish my cigarette, and you two can mingle and enjoy the buffet. There's a variety of canapés and crudités. I'm sure you'll find something to your liking."

They did. The food was scrumptious.

As they milled around, quite a few people approached Daniel to say hello. Of course he didn't recognize them, and it made for fascinating conversation. He casually quizzed them about Glynis, admitting that he didn't recall his relationship with her.

Finally, Allie and Daniel slipped off by themselves and went for a walk in the garden. He offered her his jacket since her wrap wasn't readily available.

They came to a bridge, crossed it, then stood in the shadows, evergreens scenting the air.

"Do you think Glynis was trying to throw us off track with her interest in the bartender?" she asked.

"To prove that she's not still carrying a torch for me?"

She nodded and snuggled deeper into his jacket. It was almost like being wrapped in his arms.

"I don't know. So far, none of the other guests implied that Glynis is the clingy type. If anything, they portrayed her as just the opposite."

"That doesn't mean she isn't the stalker. This could be a game to her. Watching us run around like chickens with our heads cut off."

"That's not what we're doing."

"Isn't it?"

"We're just trying to find answers, Allie."

"I wish we'd find some soon."

He escorted her back to the party, and the dragon lady threw them for another loop.

All gold and glitter, she strode up to them and said, "I've been thinking about this stalking business, and something from the past hit me."

"A corpse?" Allie asked, unable to curb her bite.

"Don't get smart or I won't tell you what I know."

Was this part of the game? Whatever it was, Daniel managed to keep his calm. But he always did. Allie couldn't deny that she was the hot-headed one.

"We're listening," he told Glynis.

She lifted her chin. The queen of the manor. "There was this odd little girl who more or less adored you."

"Who was she? How was I acquainted with her?"

"She was someone's daughter. Someone you'd completed a Warrior Society mission for. I don't remember her name. I just remember you talking about her. How shy and withdrawn she was. How she would sit in a corner at her parents' house and draw secret pictures. How she would stare at you when she thought you weren't looking."

Clearly, none of it rang a bell. Allie could tell that Daniel didn't recall a thing. For all he knew, Glynis had just fabricated the whole convenient story.

"How old was she?" he asked.

"Twelve, thirteen. The crush age. But this was about ten years ago, so she would be an adult now."

"I've known you for that long?"

"Yes, you have. We go back forever."

"You better not be sending me on a wild goose chase."

"And you better kiss my lily-white butt if she turns out to be the stalker. You, too," she informed Allie. "Now if you'll excuse me, I have other guests to tend to."

The dragon lady disappeared, leaving them to mull over what she said.

"Do you think she's lying?" Allie asked.

"I have no idea. But I'll call Rex first thing in the morning and have him look into it."

Exhausted, she sighed. "Can we go home now?"

"Absolutely." They were both more than ready to blow Glynis's pop stand.

But they only made it as far as the cloak closet when their hostess reappeared with a sprig of ribbon-wrapped mistletoe and thrust it at Allie.

"It's a party favor," she explained. "Everyone goes home with one of these tonight."

"As what? An incentive to kiss your lily-white butt?"

The dragon lady laughed, albeit clipped. "You can use it for whatever you like." She leaned in close and whispered, "When I was with Daniel during Christmastime, I tacked mistletoe above his bed. But don't go copying my moves. You aren't nearly as seductive as I am."

With that, Glynis walked away, taunting Allie with the very thing she'd yet to do.

Make love with Daniel.

"What did she say to you?" Daniel asked Allie when they got home. He'd already asked her the same question in the truck, too.

"Nothing," she responded for the second time.

"She said *something*." He glanced suspiciously at the mistletoe. "I'd rather not be around that stuff."

"Why not?" Did it subliminally remind him of Glynis? Or did it make him want to kiss Allie? She hoped it was the latter.

He provided a skewed reason. "Mistletoe is classified as a parasite, living off of other trees. Honestly, where's the value in that?"

In spite of it being a "party favor" from Glynis, Allie defended it. "There's a lot of history behind mistletoe, a lot of cultural value. In European folklore, it was one of the most magical, mysterious and sacred plants."

He didn't say anything, so she went on. "Kissing under the mistletoe started as a Greek tradition and continued throughout the world. It's also associated with Frigga, the goddess of love. It has a religious connotation, too. Some say Christ's cross was made of the wood of mistletoe."

He frowned. "Is that how mistletoe became a parasite? Was it doomed after the crucifixion?"

"According to that legend, it was. But I prefer to think of it as magical."

"Because you're a fantasy girl. Because everything is magical to you."

No, not everything. She finally came clean. "Glynis said she seduced you with it. And she told me not to copy her."

"You wouldn't need to." He took a small step in her direction. "Just looking at you seduces me."

Allie's breath lodged in her throat. Should she tell him that she wasn't wearing any panties? Or should she lift her dress and show him?

"I've been wondering if we could make it work," she said.

"Make what work?"

"Friends with benefits."

Now *his* breath seemed to lodge in *his* throat. "Have you ever made that work with anyone?"

"I did with Raven." Because the time-traveling, shape-shifting warrior had still been in love with his dead wife. He'd only slept with Allie for companionship.

Daniel didn't move forward again. He didn't invade her space. But he captured her with his unwavering gaze. "If you want to be my friend with benefits, I'm more than willing."

Of course he was. It would absolve him of having to make a commitment. But this was a serious decision for her. She was already desperately in love with him.

Now she knew how Raven had felt about his wife.

Allie glanced at the mistletoe in her hand. She set it on the coffee table, discarding it for the night. She wasn't going to make a decision based on intimidation, and certainly not by Glynis.

"You're still unsure," Daniel said.

"I'm trying not to be."

"Maybe we should just go to bed. Separately."

Maybe he was right. She knew better than to jump into something that would further complicate her already complicated heart.

"I'm sorry," she said.

"There's no need to apologize. We've been dancing

around this issue since we admitted that we're attracted to each other. And now that we know for sure that it isn't going to happen, we can relax and forget about it."

Relax, right. She was still having trouble breathing.

Coming to an agreement, they walked down the hall together. Then they paused at their respective doors and turned to look back at each other.

If time could truly stand still, this would have been one of those moments. Everything seemed to stop. Even Allie's pulse had gone dormant.

Until Daniel made a husky sound. He still wanted her. And she wanted him. So what were they doing? Going off by themselves?

"Night, Allie," he said, his voice rough.

"Night," she responded. Her voice was soft, barely audible.

He turned his doorknob, and she turned hers. He went into his room first. She entered hers and glanced back, hoping to make time stand still again. But his door was already closed.

The loss of connection all but shattered her.

She didn't want to climb into bed and touch herself. She wanted Daniel's warm, strong hands roaming her body.

So what if being with him complicated her heart? At least she would know what it was to like to have him thrusting deep inside her, making her moan, making her hot and erotic.

Anxious, Allie left her room and headed for his.

To get what she needed.

Chapter 9

Daniel's door creaked open, and there stood Allie. He didn't trust himself to speak, to utter a word.

Had she changed her mind?

God, he hoped so.

In the silence they stared at each other, and his pulse pounded at his fly. He wanted nothing more than to sweep her into his arms.

She looked like one of her paintings come to life: a fairy, a wood nymph, a mermaid, a storybook princess.

"I'm bare under my dress," she said.

The pounding got worse. He got hard, too. Brutally hard. Could she be any sexier? Could he be any more turned on?

"Totally bare," she clarified, in case he hadn't understood the first time.

Daniel wondered if he'd just died and gone to friends-with-benefits heaven. Or maybe it was hurry-up-and-make-love hell. He could barely breathe, and his mouth had gone dry.

Braless was one thing, but no panties. He'd never imagined her being that daring. Not sugar-and-spice-and-everything-nice Allie.

She reached for the hem of her dress. She seemed nervous, yet eager, too. A sweet seductress. An innocent vixen.

"Do you want me to show you?" she asked. "Do you want to see?"

He wet his parched lips. He wanted to do more than look. He wanted to eat her alive. "Only if I can put my mouth on you."

She was still clutching the hem of her dress. "You can put your mouth wherever you want."

He considered dropping to his knees, right then and there. "Then do it. Show me."

She inched up the silk, moving the fabric at an agonizing pace. He didn't blink. He refused to lose sight of her, even for a second.

Already he could see the shapely curve of her calves. Soon her thighs would be exposed. His zipper strained something fierce, and he considered undoing his pants to ease the tension. But he wasn't about to move, to risk breaking the spell.

Whoosh. She lifted her dress some more.

He held his breath, watching every lethal move she made. Finally, showed him what he wanted to see. She was soft and sexy, with a bikini wax that left little to the imagination.

"Should I take it all the way off?" she asked.

"Yes. Please," he added, sounding more polite than he felt. By now, he was fully aroused.

She peeled off her dress and tossed it aside.

Gorgeous didn't begin to describe her. Allie Whirlwind was a Lakota goddess, an Apache queen. Some of the pins that held her glorious hair came loose, making the style even messier.

He moved closer, and her stomach muscles quavered. They both knew what he intended to do.

Boom.

He fell to his knees with a thud. He looked up at her, and she looked down at him.

He parted her with his fingers and teased her with his tongue. In response, she moaned his name. Already she was wet.

He licked her some more. Foreplay, he thought. Hot, sizzling oral sex. "I could do this to you forever."

She moaned again. "Promise?"

He gripped her butt cheeks and tugged her closer, making her rock against his mouth.

Like the sweet, naughty girl she was, she widened her stance, showing him how much she liked it. Her juices flowed onto his tongue, searing him with her feminine flavor.

With his mouth still fused between her legs, he

reached up to knead her breasts. Her nipples were as ripe and dark as wild berries.

"Keep watching," he said.

Her voice was breathy. "I am."

Yes, she was. But it wasn't enough. He wanted to take it to the extreme.

"Lie down," he told her. "But leave your shoes on." Her high heels stirred a multitude of fantasies.

Daniel was never going to be the same after tonight. And neither was Allie, not after he got done with her.

She scooted onto the bed in her animal-print pumps, and he finally undid the front of his pants to relieve the tension.

Then, with his fly open, he climbed on top of her, kissing her lustfully on the lips.

The weight of his body pinned her down. She wrapped her arms around him and held tight. The kiss was warm and sinfully wet, and they went after each other in hot, hammering desperation. As their tongues danced and dived, she bucked beneath him.

The yearning was almost more than he could bear. He wanted to be inside her. But he wanted to finish what he'd started, too, and make Allie come against his mouth.

So he worked his way down: sucking on her berry-ripe nipples, blowing his breath across her stomach, toying with her belly button, doing everything within his power to arouse her.

By the time he buried his face between her legs, she was crazy with need. She tunneled her hands through his hair and moved with the rhythm of his mouth.

Writhing like the she-devil/sweet angel she was, she hiked her legs up over his shoulders, jabbing him with her shoes.

Yes, the heels he'd insisted that she wear. Nothing had ever felt so painfully good. He craved every curvaceous part of her, right down to her pretty little pumps.

She jabbed him again, and he praised the repeated pain. He couldn't think beyond the lust.

He glanced up and saw that she was watching him, as he'd instructed her to do earlier.

"Do you like being a voyeur?" he whispered against her slick, damp center.

More of her hair came loose, tangling around her breasts and falling to her waist. "Is that what it's called when you watch a friend drive you mad?"

The soft, husky way in which she said "friend" punched a shiver straight to his groin. "It is to me."

"Then I like being a voyeur." She touched herself, then sucked on the tips of her fingers, tasting the hunger between them.

Delicious frenzy.

He went down on her again. She gasped in raw excitement and begged for more.

He gave her everything he could, and she climaxed all over him.

In the heart-palpitating moment that followed,

he lifted his head, and she removed her legs from his shoulders.

"Look what I did to you," she said, trying to soothe the heel marks on his skin.

"And look what I did to you," he responded, reminding her of how wildly she'd come.

She flushed, and he leaned forward and kissed her. Deep and rough. Until they were rolling over the bed.

Locked in another bout of passion.

Allie kicked off her shoes and grabbed the front of Daniel's shirt. Pulling at the tails and tugging at the buttons, she divested him of it.

She put her hands down the front of his pants, too. She needed to touch him, to stroke him, to feel how big and hard he was.

He kissed her again, and while their tongues wrestled and their teeth clashed, she stripped him bare.

Once again, she stroked him, appreciating his masculine beauty. As an artist, she was fascinated with his hard-earned muscle and sinewy lines. As a woman, she couldn't get enough of him.

She could have a thousand orgasms and still want more. Because she loved him, she thought.

"I need you, Allie."

"I need you, too." So much more than she could tell him.

He turned his back, reached across the bed and opened the nightstand drawer, rummaging through its contents, looking for condoms.

She traced a finger down his spine. Even in this position, she *had* to touch him. His body was fast becoming her addiction.

When she slid lower, teasing his buttocks and cupping his testes from underneath, he shuddered.

But he didn't abandon his quest. He found a handful of packets in the drawer and spun around to show her.

She breathed a sigh of relief. She wasn't sure what they would have done otherwise. Allie wasn't on the Pill anymore, and she didn't have any protection. She hadn't planned on this happening.

Eager, he slipped on a condom and scooped her onto his lap.

Her heart banged against her rib cage, and he kissed her luxuriously on the mouth.

And then…

He lifted her up, and impaled her, hard and deep. He looked into her eyes, and she let the sensation of being filled by him sweep her away.

Up and down they went, riding each other like a sexual seesaw. He removed the rest of the pins from her hair, and she looped her arms around his neck.

"Does it feel as good as you remember?" she asked.

He made a hot-blooded sound. "It's better." He skimmed the sides of her body. "What's your favorite position?"

"It doesn't matter." As long as he was inside her. "What's yours?"

"I have no idea." He nuzzled the column of her

neck, nipping and kissing, being roughly affectionate. "But I want to experiment with you."

"I'm all yours." For the rest of her life, she thought. "Whenever you want me."

"I think I'm going want you all the time. Day and night. In every way imaginable." He rolled over so he could be on top.

Allie moaned her pleasure. He'd done it without breaking their connection. "You're good."

"We're good together." He placed her hands above her head, wrapping her fingers around the posts on the headboard, encouraging her to grip the wood.

It made her feel like his prisoner, his possession.

Right on cue, he swooped, taking her in a powerful kiss. Heat to heat. Shiver to shiver.

They'd left the lights burning bright. There were no shadows, no dark corners, nothing masking their joining.

Except her lie of omission.

But how could she be honest? How could she admit that she loved him?

He ended the kiss and looked into her eyes again. With a reflective expression, he touched her cheek. The calloused pads of his fingers were gently abrasive.

"You're my best friend," he said.

She struggled not to cry, not to let her emotions run away with her. He was still rocking back and forth, making incredible love to her.

Allie released the headboard and put her hands on

his chest, absorbing the warmth of his skin. She was memorizing him, too: his strong, hard pecs, his flat brown nipples.

Suddenly she wanted to paint him, the way she'd painted Raven.

No, she thought. Not like Raven.

It wouldn't be the same. She'd painted Raven from her subconscious. She would create an image of Daniel that came from her heart, immortalizing him as the warrior she loved.

She traced his scar, the part of him that spoke volumes about his character. "You're my best friend, too."

Daniel moved her hand lower, making her touch the part of him that was inside her. "Friends with benefits. What could be better than this?"

She kept quiet. She wasn't about to answer him. But it didn't matter because he wasn't expecting a response.

He maneuvered her into yet another position. He put Allie on her hands and knees and covered her like a stallion.

He was an aggressive lover. He took what he wanted, what he needed. But she had no intention of stopping him.

She needed it, too.

His penetration consumed her. She fisted the bedding and glanced toward the closet-door mirror.

She could see their reflections. Her wild-strewn hair hung down her back and her body was primitively arched. Daniel looked even more savage, with his sculpted physique and muscles glistening with sweat.

He put his mouth against her ear and whispered her name.

The tenderness in his voice contradicted the roughness of what he was doing to her. She craned her head, trying to get close enough to kiss him.

Her struggle caused a quick, shattered loss of breath. Once their mouths came together, they went mad, nearly swallowing each other whole.

He brought his hand forward, slid it between her legs and rubbed her most sensitive spot, heightening the pressure, the ache, the need.

Sensation after sensation slammed into her. She was losing her sanity, right along with the ragged remnants of her lying-to-him heart.

"Come for me," he said.

"I am. Oh, God, I am." The tremors had already begun, rushing through her blood and shocking her skin.

She gazed at the mirror again. She really was a voyeur. She couldn't get enough of seeing them together.

Hot. Naked. Desperate.

By now, Daniel was plowing his fingers through her hair and biting the back of her neck.

Relentless, he kept his hand between her legs. Rubbing. Stroking. He was moving inside her, too, pushing toward his own raging climax.

When it happened, they exploded together, and Allie

knew that she was in trouble. Making love with Daniel had changed her. Her attachment to him had grown instantly stronger, imminently more dangerous.

He released her, and they turned to face each other. She wanted to weep for her foolishness, then climb all over him and do it again.

He was so perfect, she thought. So primal. So male. His hair fell across his forehead in sex-tousled disarray, and he was still half hard, even after he got out of bed to dispose of the condom. It wouldn't take much to bring him back to full speed.

But she didn't do it. When he returned, she kept her hands to herself.

Still, was it any wonder that she wanted him again? Or that she was afraid of how she felt?

She loved him even more now.

He settled onto a pillow, making sure she was beside him.

She snuggled into his embrace, preparing to sleep in his arms, to keep her emotions hidden.

If she showed signs of regret, of fear, of uncertainty, she knew that he would blame himself for damaging her fragile psyche and never touch her again.

And that would be far worse than never having been with him at all.

Chapter 10

In the morning, Daniel watched Allie sleep. He was tempted to wake her with a kiss, but a kiss would never be enough. If he put his mouth against hers, he would want more.

He was still naked and so was she.

She looked tousled, that was for sure. But what did he expect after last night? He'd all but devoured her.

Had his sexual appetite always been that strong?

Gingerly, he moved a strand of Allie's hair away from her face, smoothing her rumpled appearance. She'd made him feel like a starving kid in a candy store. Even now, he was fighting a sweet tooth.

Damn, but he wanted to do her again.

Before she woke up and caught him staring at her,

he got out of bed and grabbed the robe from the back of his bathroom door. Then he went into the living room to call Rex.

The other man answered instantly. Rex was always on his toes, always prepared to work. But somehow he managed to play hard, too.

"What's up?" the P.I. asked.

Besides getting laid for the first time in Lord only knew how long? Plenty, Daniel thought. "We went to Glynis's shindig last night."

"How'd it go?"

"Strange," he admitted, glancing at the coffee table, where Allie had discarded the party favor mistletoe. "Glynis gave us some information I want you to check out."

"Shoot," Rex said.

Daniel proceeded to repeat the story, and the P.I. promised to get on it right away.

Within minutes, they ended the call, leaving Daniel thinking about Allie again. He returned to the bedroom and sat on the edge of the bed. She was still asleep.

Would she enjoy the Snow White treatment of being awakened by a kiss? Not that he wanted to model her after a fairy-tale character, especially with the whole poison-apple thing. Being threatened by a stalker was enough. She didn't need a witch threatening her, too. Been there, done that, he thought.

Before he got the opportunity to kiss her, her eyelids fluttered and she woke up on her own. She squinted for a moment, and once she got acclimated to the morning light, they gazed at each other.

"Hi," he said.

"Hi," she responded, just as simply.

After that, neither of them said anything else. Was this typical morning-after behavior? Since he didn't have any memories to go on, he couldn't compare it to past experiences.

Daniel wanted to climb back into bed with her, but he stayed where he was, seated on the edge of the mattress.

As for Allie, she held the sheet tightly against her breasts, as if she'd suddenly become aware of being naked underneath.

Was she self-conscious because he was wearing his robe? He would've gladly ditched it for her, but the awkwardness hadn't gone away.

To combat the silence, he said, "I called Rex."

She still held the sheet a little too tight. "What did he say?"

"That he would follow through on it."

"So all we have to do is wait?"

"And keep busy."

"Doing what?"

As soon as the question was out of her mouth, the awkwardness got even more palpable. He could've reached right out and grabbed the thickness in the air.

Determined to end the discomfort he said, "Truthfully? We could quit acting like last night didn't happen and go jump in the shower together."

She broke out in a smile, and so did he, grateful that she appreciated his candor.

"You were almost a virgin," she teased.

"Because I don't remember being with anyone but you? Almost only counts in horseshoes and hand grenades," he reminded her. "Come on, Allie." His sweet, sweet friend. "Get naked with me."

She teased him again. "Are you sure you don't want to make gingerbread houses instead?"

"Sorry, Christmas con. It's naked or nothing."

"I'm already bare." She loosened her hold on the sheet, letting it slip. Not all the way, but enough to expose a luscious burst of cleavage and a hint of areola.

Captivated, he leaned over and kissed her, slipping his tongue past her lips. Slowly at first, savoring the feeling, then faster, feeding his fantasy, until his pulse points, every last one of them, screamed for salvation.

She tossed her arms around his neck, and he scooped her up and carried her to the tub, grabbing a condom on the way.

He set her in the shower, turned on the water and watched it sluice down her body.

Beads of wetness clung to her nipples and ran in rivulets from her navel to her bikini wax. She didn't have tan lines. She was naturally dark all over.

When she ducked her head under the rain-like spray, soaking her long, shadowy tresses, he disrobed and joined her.

"Fearless." She used his Warrior Society nickname, while the shower gathered mist.

He pressed his nakedness against hers, and she fondled his big gun salute.

She dropped to her knees, and his heart threatened to jackhammer its way out of his bullet-scarred chest.

"You don't have to do that," he said, as water pummeled his back.

She looked up at him. All wet and mermaid-like. "Do you remember what it feels like?"

"Not specifically." His sexual memories were lumped together in urges, in instincts.

"Then why don't you want me to do it?"

His heart hammered again. Or maybe it had never stopped. "I didn't say I didn't want you to. I said you didn't have to."

"If it's my choice, then I'm doing it."

She kissed him softly, there at the tip, before she took him in her mouth, making him reiterate that she was his best friend. His very best friend.

In the entire world.

He tangled his hands in her sopped hair and looked down at her beautiful face. "I'll try not to..."

She stopped pleasuring him, but only long enough to respond, "It's okay if you do."

"I'll still try not to." He was his doing damnedest to be a gentleman, even while she was on her knees for him.

"I could make you," she challenged.

His breath chopped. The steam was getting thicker, and he was painfully hard. "Yeah, you could." He wasn't going to deny that she had that kind of power over him.

He delved deeper into her hair and watched the way her cheeks hollowed as she sucked.

The more she worked him, the more he fought a climax. She kept stealing glances, and the eye contact intensified the intimacy.

He didn't care if he never remembered anyone but her. She was all that mattered. Allie was the only woman he would die for, the only woman who was killing him right now.

When she took him all way to the back of her throat, he gave himself a moment to breathe, then yanked her up and pushed her against the shower wall.

He wanted to look into her eyes when he came, so he kept her right where she was.

Pinned against the tile.

Daniel grabbed the condom. The water was still running, splashing off his body and onto hers.

Once he sheathed himself, he lowered his head to lick her nipples, to arouse her with cherry-sweet foreplay. He used his fingers inside her, too. Making sure she was ready for him.

She was. Ready and willing.

Since she was tall enough to accept his penetration where they stood, he went for it. With one aggressive thrust, he was inside her.

He moved, hilt deep, and she dug her nails into his shoulders. Kissing and biting, they made cat-scratch love.

While he pumped his hips, he lifted her up, locking her legs around him. It was an acrobatic maneuver for both of them, but it made the rocking motion that much wilder.

His blood roared in his veins. His vision blurred, too, but he kept his gaze fixed on hers. She was all he wanted to see, all he wanted to feel.

He didn't know who came first. His only awareness was that they convulsed, over and over, until their breathing shattered and they were dizzily spent.

He put her back on her feet, and she went slack in his arms. The shower was like a sauna.

Too hot. Too steamy. Too damp.

He turned off the spigot and discarded the rubber.

In the quiet, he kissed her, then rested his forehead against hers. One of these times, he was going to be romantic with her, instead of ravishing her like an animal.

But for now, he handed her a couple of towels. She wrapped one around her hair, turban style, and used the other on her body. Daniel dried off, too.

Luckily the silence wasn't awkward. It was actually quite companionable, especially when they smiled softly at each other.

Soon Allie retreated to the guest bathroom to finish getting ready. He stayed where he was to complete his morning routine.

When he reentered his bedroom, he noticed that

their clothes from last night were scattered all over the floor.

He picked up her red dress and felt the silk run through his fingers. He draped it over his bureau and looked for her shoes, only finding one of them. The other was nowhere to be seen.

But he remembered how she looked in them. Sultry images crowded his mind.

He got dressed and discovered her other high heel under the bed. He placed the leopard-print pump with its mate.

Since it was breakfast time, Daniel headed for the kitchen and started a pot of coffee. By the time Allie arrived, a roasted aroma scented the air.

"Do you feel like cooking?" he asked.

"No. Do you?"

"Not today." He hadn't mastered his culinary skills yet. "We could have cereal."

"That's sounds good."

He went to the cabinet, and she went to the fridge. She looked fresh and pretty. Her damp hair was fastened in a ponytail, and she wore a light coat of mascara and clear lip gloss.

But was she wearing a bra or panties? He took a closer look. Yes, on the bra. The panties, he couldn't be sure.

Allie retrieved the milk, and Daniel held up two cereal boxes. "Which one do you want?"

She pointed to the brand that snapped, crackled and popped, and he joined her at the table.

Halfway through the meal, the phone rang. He answered it, and she mouthed, "Is it Rex?"

He shook his head and informed her that it was Detective Bell. The cop wanted to talk to her.

Daniel handed her the phone and listened to her side of the conversation.

"A wig?" she said. "No. I don't have one." She paused, then answered the detective's next question. "No, my sister doesn't, either."

The discussion was short, and Daniel got the gist of it. Some of the hair samples that had been collected at her loft had come from a wig the same length and color as Allie's hair.

After she hung up, she turned toward him. "You heard?"

He nodded. "Does Bell have a theory about the wig?"

"He said the stalker was probably wearing it to draw less attention to herself. If someone saw her going up the stairs to my loft, they might've thought she was me. But he also said that she might have wanted to know how it felt to look like me."

"No one would ever think Susan's sister was you. Her figure is too full."

"Glynis might pass from a distance, with bronzing makeup and my style of clothes. But that's a bit of a stretch."

"It could have been the girl Glynis mentioned."

"If she's even real."

Daniel blew out a tight breath. He could only hope

that Glynis had been telling the truth. For now, the stalker seemed like a phantom.

And that made protecting Allie seem just as elusive.

For the next two days, Daniel seemed even more protective of Allie. Was it because they were lovers? Had that made him more of a bodyguard? Or was it because Rex hadn't uncovered any information about the girl Glynis had mentioned?

Whatever the case, he remained by her side.

She turned to look at him. They'd just carried groceries in from his truck and were preparing to unpack the bags. They planned on cooking together later. She was going to teach him to make stuffed bell peppers, using ground beef for him and veggie crumbles for her.

"Are you still going to want to hang around with me when this is all over?" she asked.

He scanned the length of her. "You're kidding right?"

No, she thought, I'm not.

"Allie, why would I let you go?"

Now that they were lovers? His meaning was clear. "You wouldn't, I guess."

"Damn right, I wouldn't. Our friendship isn't going to end."

"It will if one of us starts needing a committed relationship."

He cocked his head. He was frowning. "With each other or with someone else?"

With each other, she thought. But she said, "Either, or."

"Why worry about that now?" He started unloading a bag of frozen food. "Why mess with success?"

Unrequited love wasn't success. Allie ached inside. But she put on a brave front. "You're right. It's just the dreamy side of me talking."

"The fantasy girl." He came forward to kiss her, to press his lips lightly against hers.

But he was pressing a carton of ice cream against her, too. She shivered from the cold.

He stepped back, realizing what he'd done. "Sorry." He flashed a sheepish smile. "At least it's your favorite flavor."

She smiled, too. At least he knew what her favorite flavor was. She doubted that there was another woman he could say that about.

After all of the food was put away, he asked, "Do you want to get out of the house for a while?"

"And go where?"

"I don't know." He thought it over for a moment. "How about a park or a beach?"

"A beach," she decided. She loved the sand and the surf, even on breezy winter days.

He rattled off a list of locations. "Manhattan, Malibu, Redondo, Santa Monica, Venice or Zuma?"

Allie considered her options. "Let's do Venice." She wanted to be in a lively setting, where she wouldn't dwell too deeply on love or darkness or death or any of the other things that continued to plague her mind.

"I'm game." He was ready to go.

She grabbed her sweater, and they headed out the door.

Once they arrived, they drove around and searched for a parking spot. Although Venice Beach was a tourist summer spot, it bustled during the holiday season, too. Vendors peddled their wares and homeowners decorated their canal-front properties.

The city limits were decorated with commissioned artwork, too. As a mural of Jim Morrison on the side of a building came into view, Allie reveled in the culture.

She turned to Daniel. "Can you imagine what this place was like when he lived here?"

"Crazy, I'm sure. It's still kind of whacky."

"That's what makes it so great."

"I think so, too." He glanced at Morrison's half-naked body. "Who painted that?"

"Rip Cronk. He's amazing. His work is all over this town." She studied Daniel's profile, and the urge to immortalize him came back. Only this time, she expressed her feelings out loud. "I'd like to paint you like that."

He shot her an incredulous look. "On the side of a building?"

"No. In my loft. I have some free wall space."

"That's all you need. A big-ass painting of me. It wouldn't go with your other mural."

"Yes, it would." Her other mural featured unicorns, fairies and an armor-clad knight slaying a dragon. "I already told you that you're my real-life knight."

"What if you stop feeling that way about me?"

"That won't happen. You'll always be one of my heroes."

"Because I got shot for you?" He stopped at a red light. "I'm a man with an empty mind, Allie. I'm not a good subject for your art."

"I'll give you memories. I'll paint them inside your head."

He turned onto a narrow side street and found a parking place, wedging his truck between two other cars. "But those memories wouldn't be real."

Not unless she was able to create magic with her art, the way she used to. But Allie doubted that she could. Lately, her life had been grounded in deep, dark reality.

They exited the truck and took to the streets. She didn't mention the painting again and neither did he.

As soon as they got to the boardwalk, Daniel's cell phone rang. It was Rex, and he wanted to meet with them to discuss the girl Glynis had told them about.

According to the P.I., she existed.

Right down to her schizophrenic disorder.

Chapter 11

Daniel and Allie sat on a bench outside a surf shop and waited for Rex. To keep themselves occupied, they watched the boardwalk activity.

Venice was loud and messy. In the summer, the regulars consisted of hippie types, artists, tourists, bodybuilders, dog lovers, skateboarders and homeless people. The winter crowd was much the same, except the sun worshippers were more clothed than usual.

Daniel thought it was an interesting place to spend the afternoon. But Rex's call had shaken his and Allie's emotions. Both were anxious for more information.

"I wish he'd hurry up and get here," she said.

"At least this place is entertaining." He gestured

to a nearby coffee cart. "Do you want something to drink?"

"Sure. I'll take a latte."

"That sounds good to me, too." He stood up. "I'll be right back, okay? But don't move from this bench. Stay where I can see you."

"I will." She smiled a little.

He waited in a short line, then ordered their drinks. He got a couple of cranberry muffins, too. Naturally, he kept glancing back at Allie.

When he returned, she took her coffee and accepted one of the muffins. He settled beside her. He heard a raven caw, and the bird's voice gave him a quick start.

He turned toward the sound. "In Haida folklore, Raven is a trickster, a mythological demigod. But I guess I've told you that before."

"Yes, when we first met. I wish you remembered my Raven."

"So do I." A shard of envy jabbed his gut. "But he isn't yours anymore."

"He never really was. He always belonged to his wife." She sipped her latte. "At least you've seen the painting I did of him."

Yes, he'd seen it: a powerful image of a warrior with piercing eyes and long flowing hair.

"He admired you, Daniel. He trusted you to locate the talisman that saved him."

He watched the bird that had cawed. It sat high atop a telephone pole. "Maybe this raven is trying to tell us something."

"Like what?"

The bird looked down at him, and Daniel wondered if it was a common raven or a mythical one. Sometimes you couldn't tell. "Maybe he's trying to tell us that the stalker is a trickster, too."

Allie picked at her muffin, dropping crumbs on her lap. "She's certainly tricked us so far." Her attention shifted to a tall, broad figure coming their way. "Rex is here."

The P.I. smiled at a pretty girl as she passed, and Daniel shook his head. Rex Sixkiller had a causal way about him. Charming, Daniel supposed, to women anyway.

If Rex lived on the edge, he didn't let it show. But at least he had a permit to carry a concealed weapon. Daniel, like most California civilians, was unarmed.

Not that he hadn't broken the law for his Warrior Society missions. Daniel was an accomplished thief. In spite of the amnesia, he remembered how to bypass security systems and pick locks.

But this thing with Allie was different. As far as he knew, he'd never volunteered to protect anyone before.

Rex greeted them and scooted onto the bench, sitting next to Allie. The P.I. shifted his gaze between them. "Something's changed between you two."

Allie had the grace to blush, and Daniel scowled. The other man was way too observant. He'd sniffed out the sex instantly. But that was probably a skill that went with his job, following around cheating spouses and whatnot.

Regardless, Daniel didn't like it.

"Just stick to the case," he told Rex.

The other man shrugged, and a serious conversation ensued.

"Her name is Ann Kangee," Rex said, referring to the girl Glynis had mentioned.

"Kangee?" Daniel started.

Rex cocked his head at a curious angle. "Does that name ring a bell?"

"No. But it means raven in Lakota," Daniel said.

"Oh, my God." Allie released a sharp breath. "You're right, it does. Kanga, Kange, Kangee, Kangie, Kangi, Kangy. They're all variants of raven."

Rex went quiet, but he seemed stunned, too. He was aware of the raven connection. All of the Warrior Society knew about Allie's shape-shifter lover and about Daniel's belief that ravens were tricksters.

"I wonder if it's an omen," Rex said.

"I think it is." Daniel glanced up, scanning the telephone pole for the bird that had been watching him, but it was gone. "Ravens keep coming into our lives, even in the form of Ann's name."

"Then let me tell you about her." Rex cleared his throat and continued. "She's twenty-three and lives off a trust fund she received from her maternal grandparents. She's a mixed-blood. Native father. Anglo mother."

"Does she have a history of violence?" Daniel asked.

"No."

"But she has a mental disorder?"

"Yes. Schizophrenia is characterized by abnormalities in the perception or expression of reality. Since this is such a sensitive issue, I took the liberty of calling her parents."

Daniel didn't mind Rex's intervention, not if it helped. "How'd that go?"

"Her mother insists that she's harmless. That she would never threaten anyone."

"What about the father?"

"I didn't talk to him."

"Did her mother say anything else?"

"She admitted that Ann gets obsessed with celebrities and that she had overly amorous feelings for you when she was younger."

"How does Ann feel about me now?"

"It's tough to say. She's been gone for two months."

"Gone?" This from Allie.

"She lives with her parents, but every so often, she goes off by herself, disappearing purposely. They used to search for her, but now they just let her be. Eventually she comes home on her own."

Allie spoke again. "How difficult can she be to find?"

Rex frowned. "Difficult enough. She lives off cash, so there's no paper trail to follow."

Damn it, Daniel thought. One step forward, two steps back. "I'd like to talk to her parents myself."

"I already told the mother that you'd be contacting them. According to her, they have fond memories of you. You helped the father recover a medicine bundle that was stolen from his ancestors. You're a hero in their eyes."

"I'll be kind about their daughter." But he wouldn't stop pushing for answers. He needed to know if Ann was the stalker. "Has she ever been institutionalized?"

Rex shook his head. "She's considered a high functioning schizophrenic."

"But she still has a tenuous grasp on reality?" It sounded complicated to Daniel. "Glynis said that she liked to draw. Did you ask her mother if she was a good artist? If she was into comic books? Or if she favored wigs?"

"I didn't discuss those elements. I figured you'd be doing a complete interview."

Yes, he would, with Allie by his side. The woman whose safety depended on it.

After Rex left, Daniel called the Kangees, but they weren't available until tomorrow, leaving him and Allie with another full day of waiting.

They decided to return to his truck. They didn't want to stay at the beach. Venice was too loud for their solemn mood.

As Daniel unlocked the doors, Allie reached for what appeared to be a handbill on the windshield. But when she glanced at the white sheet of paper, she gasped.

He didn't ask what was wrong. He simply rushed over to the passenger side of the vehicle where she stood. Although she held tightly to the paper, her hands were shaking.

Oh, God, he thought.

While they'd been at the beach, the stalker had made another threat. This time it was a comic-book-style rendering of Allie in a plain wooden coffin, the lid open for viewing.

"Allie in a box," she said, reminding him of the night she'd slept in his arms, fearful of nightmares, of seeing herself in a coffin.

And now she had.

Before Daniel pried the drawing from her fingers, he called Detective Bell.

While the police were en route, he said, "This isn't an omen. This isn't going to happen."

"How did she know it was my worst nightmare?"

"She didn't. She couldn't have." Was that the best he could do? The best he could say? Daniel had never felt more inept. "She just drew you in the next stage." The first drawing was death. The second was the burial. In a twisted way, it made storybook sense.

"Do you think Ann is the stalker?" she asked. "Do you think she did this?"

He looked into Allie's eyes and realized that she was trying to temper the fear by having a logical discussion, by focusing on the investigation.

"Do you?" she asked again.

"Yes," he responded. "It seems possible that Ann is the stalker. But I can't help wonder what would trigger it after all these years."

"Maybe it was the shooting. Maybe she read about

you in the paper, and her old feelings came back. Something like that could have renewed her childhood crush and made her start obsessing about you again."

"You're right. It very well could have. Plus, she's been missing for two months, about the same time I got out of the hospital."

"Maybe she's been watching you since your coma."

"And she doesn't like me being friends with you?"

"I'm the only woman in your life. It stands to reason that she would consider me a threat. Not to mention that you were shot because of me."

"We might be onto something here." Or they could be way off base and be blaming an innocent girl. "Hopefully we'll be able to figure things out once we talk to her parents."

"I feel bad for them, having to defend their mentally ill child."

"Me, too. But her psychosis could be the key to all of this. As far as we know, our other suspects don't struggle with reality."

"Glynis likens herself to Bettie Page."

"Yeah, but that seems like vanity."

"Rather than insanity?" Allie sighed. "Can you imagine how Glynis is going to gloat if she turns out to be right?"

Daniel made a face. "We're not kissing her lily-white butt."

Allie scrunched her nose, mirroring his expression, and they sputtered into laughter.

A moment later they went quiet. Too quiet. Their situation wasn't funny.

"I wonder what Ann looks like," Allie said.

"We'll have to ask her parents for a recent picture. We'll have to tell Detective Bell about her, too." He frowned at the coffin drawing, wishing the police would hurry up and get there.

"Maybe Bell will locate a witness," she said.

Someone who saw the stalker? "Maybe." But Daniel doubted that with all the bustling activity in Venice, a woman placing a "handbill" on a solitary vehicle would have garnered attention.

"I wish this would end."

"It will," he told her, praying that he spoke the truth. "It'll end soon."

Christmas was right around the corner, and after the holiday, he and Allie would be returning to work. How vulnerable would she be then? Without him by her side?

"I'm going to do some research on schizophrenia in conjunction with stalking," he said. "If Ann is the culprit, it might help us second-guess her."

In response, Allie touched his arm, making a physical connection. He took it a step further, pulling her tight against him.

She went pliant in his arms, but he didn't gentle his hold. Daniel couldn't bear to let go. Even when the police arrived, he stayed close to her.

Very, very close.

* * *

The Kangees lived in an apartment in Old Pasadena, above the trendy restaurant they owned.

Old Pasadena wasn't as colorful as Venice, but it was still a tourist attraction, hosting the New Year's Day Tournament of Roses Parade every year. Soon Colorado Boulevard would be flooded with flower-covered floats.

Daniel and Allie stood outside the Santa Arroyo Eatery, preparing to walk around to the side of the building.

Was Allie as uncomfortable as he was? He suspected that she was. Neither of them relished the idea of accusing Ann of a crime, at least not to her parents' faces.

But the research Daniel had done last night confirmed that Ann could be stalker material.

According to a pertinent article he'd read, wives and girlfriends were often the target of female stalkers because of the stalker's infatuation with the husband or boyfriend.

These types of delusional stalkers fell into the intimacy-seeking profile, believing that the husband or boyfriend was their soul mate.

Was that how Ann saw him? As a soul mate?

He glanced at Allie. "Ready?"

She nodded, and they headed for the brick stairs that led to the Kangees's apartment. Once they reached the top, Daniel rang the bell.

Carolyn Kangee answered the door. She was a refined, carefully coiffed, middle-aged blonde in jeans and a white blouse. Her jewelry rivaled Allie's. Ann's mother favored blue bling.

"Daniel?" she said. "I wouldn't have recognized you."

"I know. I've changed." He introduced Allie, and the other woman gave her an anxiety-ridden smile. She was as uncomfortable as they were.

Why? Because deep down she knew that her daughter was capable of being a stalker?

Carolyn invited them inside and Ron Kangee came forward. He greeted Daniel and Allie in Lakota, respecting the Native roots they shared.

Ron was a stocky man with graying hair, deep-set eyes and broad features. He looked hard and rough next to his fair and delicate wife. But nonetheless, they seemed well suited, especially in the urban setting. Old Pasadena was a melting pot of ethnicities.

Daniel suspected that Carolyn's family had provided the money for the restaurant, just as they'd provided Ann's trust fund.

The Kangees offered Daniel and Allie a seat, and they gathered in the living room. The spacious apartment boasted a view of the city, hardwood floors and antique furnishings.

"I apologize that I don't remember you," Daniel said, starting the conversation.

"It's okay. We understand." Carolyn folded her hands on her lap. "We heard about your injury."

"From whom?"

"Ann read about the museum shooting in the paper and called the hospital to check on your progress. She discovered that you'd lost your memory." Carolyn twisted her fingers together. "She was upset when she heard the news. It broke her heart to think that you'd forgotten her. But she's sensitive about those sorts of things."

"Tell me about my relationship with her. How did she perceive me?"

"She adored you, but she was just a child. A young girl with a crush. It was innocent enough."

Back then, Daniel thought. But what about now? "Did she discuss her drawings with me?"

"Goodness, no." Carolyn continued to answer his questions, but her husband remained quiet. "She barely spoke to you. But she did create a comic book with you as a superhero."

Daniel heard Allie suck in her breath, but he didn't glance her way. "A comic book? What inspired that?"

"You did. You told her that the Warrior Society called you Fearless after Fearless Fly, so she drew up her own version of you as a fearless superhero."

"Really?" He kept his voice strong and steady. "Who did I save?"

"Why, Ann, of course. She put herself in the book." Carolyn frowned. "I know how that probably sounds to you. But she did that sort of thing all of time. She made comic books with celebrities in them, too. But she never bothered anyone. She just created her own fantasies."

"Allie received threatening drawings," Daniel said. "Like pages from a horror comic. I have copies if you wouldn't mind taking a look."

Defensive, the mother lifted her chin. "Ann isn't into that horror junk. That isn't her style."

"I'd like to see them," Ron said, and received a scowl from his wife.

Daniel removed the photocopies from his pocket and handed it to Ann's father. The other man studied the comics carefully.

"I've never seen her do anything this dark," he said. "But that doesn't mean she didn't draw them." He turned to his wife. "Annie is ill, Mama. We both know that. And these people know it, too."

Carolyn's eyes got watery, and she repeated her statement from earlier. "But her delusions have never been dangerous."

"How can we be sure of what's going on in her mind? Especially when she disappears the way she does?" Ron addressed Daniel. "I know of families who have children like ours. Functioning schizophrenics who suddenly do something violent. It's always scared me."

Carolyn defended the disorder. "Most schizophrenics aren't violent."

"I know," her husband said. "But what if Annie drew these? What if she's having macabre thoughts?" Silent, he returned the deathly drawings to Daniel.

A moment later, Daniel shattered the quiet. "The woman who broke into Allie's loft was wearing a wig. She might have been disguising herself to look like Allie. Does Ann seem capable of that?"

Ron responded, "Annie loves to playact. She took quite a few theater arts and film classes at community college. So I suppose she could successfully mimic someone else. She's about Allie's height and weight, too."

Daniel decided this was a good time to ask for a picture. "Do you have a recent photograph of Ann we could have?"

"I'll print one from the computer." Ron left the room, and Carolyn sat there, stiff and emotional and clearly worried about their daughter.

When Ron returned, Daniel studied the young woman's image. She was a combination of both parents, with medium brown hair, greenish-gold eyes and mixed features.

He handed it to Allie. She stared at it for the longest time, then said, "I think I've seen Ann before. She seems familiar."

"How familiar?" Daniel asked.

Allie shook her head. She didn't seem to know, but regardless, she couldn't take her eyes off the picture.

Chapter 12

On Christmas Eve, Daniel and Allie drove around and dropped off gingerbread houses to Allie's friends, something she did every year. It was a bright and festive night, but Daniel's mood was dark and worrisome.

Nothing new had developed in the case. They hadn't located Ann Kangee, even with her parents' help, and no matter how many times Allie looked at Ann's picture, she couldn't define her familiarity. Nonetheless, Allie remained convinced that she'd seen her before.

But where? Daniel wondered. At the market? At the bank? At everyday places where Allie had caught unaware glimpses of her?

Detective Bell considered Ann a "person of

interest," which meant that she was someone he would like to speak with or investigate further in connection with the crime.

Yeah, Daniel thought, you and me both.

After the final delivery was made, Daniel and Allie returned to his place to indulge in the treats she'd made for them to enjoy, which included gingerbread men and eggnog.

What the hell, Daniel decided, as they sat in front of the tree. He might as well bite the smiling head off of a cookie and swig down a drink spiked with cognac and whiskey.

Allie put Christmas music on the CD player, and he pondered what a strange and wondrous creature she was. It didn't matter that she was in the midst of being stalked, she still loved the holidays.

"Bing Crosby?" he asked.

She dipped a ladle into the eggnog and spooned up a cup for him. "*Holiday Inn* is one of my favorite movies."

"I thought this was the title song from *White Christmas*."

She handed him the eggnog. "It is. But it originated in *Holiday Inn*. Irving Berlin won an Academy Award that year for the best original song."

Fascinated, he got comfortable on the sofa. Allie was a wealth of trivia. She sat next to him and nibbled on a gingerbread man, and they listened to the music.

"Do you want to open our presents to each other tonight?" she asked.

"Sure. Okay." He agreed, even if exchanging gifts made him nervous. He wasn't totally confident about what he'd bought her.

Another song came on. This time, Bruce Springsteen belted out *Santa Claus is Coming to Town.* Apparently the CD was a collection of various artists from different eras.

Allie knelt in front of the tree. "Which present is mine?"

Daniel joined her. "Those two." He hadn't put tags on any of them. "The other one is for my dad."

"This is yours." She handed him a small box wrapped in gold paper and decorated with a red bow.

He didn't like receiving presents anymore than he liked giving them. The whole ritual made him uneasy. But he was trying to get past his Christmas crankiness and see the holiday through Allie's eyes.

"You go ahead," he told her.

"Does it matter which one I open first?" She seemed excited that he'd gotten her two gifts. Everything about her sparkled.

"No. It's your choice."

She went for the bigger box and tore into it like a kid, discovering a stuffed toy inside. She petted the plush black kitten. "Oh, Daniel. He's adorable."

"I figured he could keep you company until Sam comes home." He skimmed her cheek, loving the softness of her skin. "I know how much you miss her."

Allie leaned over to kiss him, and she tasted

sweet and intoxicating. He wanted to scoop her up and carry her to bed, but they hadn't finished unwrapping presents.

"Your turn," she said.

Daniel opened his gift, which was a stunning turquoise rosary. He fingered the beads and got a feeling of déjà vu. "This means something to me, doesn't it?"

She nodded. "You brought a rosary just like it to the museum. But instead of holding on to it for yourself, you gave it to Raven. He promised to return it, but somewhere along the way, it got lost."

"Thank you, Allie." He pressed the beads against his heart. "It's beautiful."

"Turquoise beads were used by the Apache as protection against witchcraft, but you weren't aware of that when you offered it to Raven. The rosary you gave him was the one you used in church every Sunday."

"And now I'll use this one." He kissed her the way she'd kissed him, and the lights on the tree blinked, making the moment even more Christmassy.

When they separated, he said, "I was planning on going to midnight Mass tonight. Do you want to go with me?"

"Does it matter that I'm not Catholic?"

"Not at all."

"Then I'd love to."

He reached for her other present. "You still have one more gift."

She grinned and ripped into it. Then she gasped. He'd given her a hand-carved jewelry box decorated with a mermaid.

"She reminds me of you," he said. "Her hair is made of onyx, and her eyes are black pearls."

"Thank you, Daniel. I love it. I absolutely love it." She put her head on his shoulder, and he held her.

"Come to bed with me, Allie."

She looked up. "I thought you were taking me to church."

"I am. But we have time." For now, he needed to be naked with her. "I want to make romantic love with you."

"Then I'm all yours." She reached for his hand, and they entered the bedroom.

He turned off the lights and lit several tall, white candles. He lit a bundle of sage, too, and put the sacred herb in a conch shell where it purified the air.

She removed her clothes, and Daniel got undressed, too. He tugged at his garments much more roughly than she did. Allie stripped in a sleek yet shy way. Innocently sensual, he thought. It was part of her DNA.

Once they were naked, he reminded himself not to hurry.

They reclined on the bed and kissed, and he caressed her, sliding his hands up and down. She was as enchanting as the mermaid he'd given her.

"You could have come from the sea," he said.

"I feel like I'm dreaming."

"Maybe we both are." For now, they'd suspended reality. There was no danger. No stalker. No anxiety. There was only the luxury of each other.

Daniel slipped his hand between her legs and stroked her. She smiled softly, dazzling him.

He considered asking her to move in with him permanently, to stay with him forever, but he was only caught up in the moment, in the romance he was determined to create.

Allie made a kittenish sound, and he brought her to climax. In his imagination, the ocean lapped at her body, bathing her in moonlight.

Her eyes were closed, and he was able to watch her without reserve. Her hair curtained the pillow, and her lips were full and enticing.

He leaned forward and kissed her, making her climax even more idyllic. She sighed, even as she shuddered.

Finally, she opened her eyes and looked at him. "What are you doing to me?"

"Making you feel good." They both spoke in hushed tones.

She trailed a finger down the center of his body, stopping to tease his navel. "I like making you feel good, too."

His stomach muscles jumped. "It's strange that we haven't known each other for very long, yet we're so close." He paused to acknowledge the past. "But we've been through a lot together."

She stilled her hand. “I’m sorry you lost your memory.”

“It isn’t your fault.”

“Sometimes I feel like it is.”

“Don’t talk like that. Don’t blame yourself.”

“I know I shouldn’t, but—”

“Shh.” They’d gotten off track, letting reality seep in. “Tonight is our escape, Allie.”

He kissed her once again, and they rolled across the bed, tangling the sheets and pressing their bodies unbearably close.

Needing more, Daniel secured a condom from the nightstand.

“Let me put it on you,” she said.

He wasn’t about to say no. He wanted nothing more than for Allie to touch him.

She tore open the packet and put the protection to good use, climbing onto his lap.

As she impaled herself, his heart struck his chest. When their gazes locked, he circled her waist, lifting her up and bringing her back down.

With each thrust, Daniel shivered, and so did she.

Intensifying the connection, he shifted positions and reentered her, the penetration hard and languidly deep. She wrapped her legs around him, and he rocked her body with his.

“More,” she whispered.

Yes, *more.*

Every breath, every nuance, every warm, willing

caress fueled his fantasy. Together, they inhaled the scent of sage and white wax.

Sexual purity, he thought.

On Christmas Eve.

On Christmas day, Allie prepared a meal with Daniel's father, sharing the kitchen and enjoying each other's company. She made vegetarian dishes to accompany the traditional turkey, mashed potatoes and chestnut stuffing Ernie had prepared.

After dinner, they gathered in the living room and ate pumpkin pie. Aside from Ernie, their guests included Kyle and Joyce Prescott.

Kyle, a half-blood Apache, was the founder of the Warrior Society. At six foot four, with blunt-cut hair and raw, rugged muscle, he never failed to kick some serious ass. His pretty blonde wife was just as tough. She was a Special Sections homicide detective who'd helped put Allie's serial killer mother behind bars.

Of course at the present time, Joyce was on maternity leave from her job. Her belly swelled with a baby girl her rough-and-ready husband had planted deep within her womb.

Allie couldn't help but watch the other couple. They were openly in love, and she admired their dedication to each other. As much as she hated to admit it, she envied them, too.

They sat side-by-side on the sofa, and every so often, Kyle would place his hand on his wife's stomach, waiting for the baby to kick, and grinning like a fool when it did.

Allie wanted kids someday. Lots of them.

"We're going to my family's house later," Joyce said.

"For a second Christmas dinner." Kyle chuckled. "But we can handle it. We're eating for two."

"We?" his wife queried.

Kyle shrugged and laughed. Allie and Ernie laughed as well, but Daniel seemed distracted.

"Son?" Ernie said. "Are you okay?"

"I'm just..." The younger Deer Runner put his uneaten dessert on an end table.

"Thinking about the stalker?" Joyce asked, her instincts on sudden alert.

Daniel nodded and turned to look at Allie. Their gazes met and held, and she got fluttery inside. But he always affected her that way.

"Don't worry," she said, before the silence got too awkward. "I'll be all right." She knew he was concerned about her going back to work. "It'll be good for me to be with my students again."

"I'd rather keep you with me."

Touched by his sentiment, she smiled. She wanted to crawl into his lap and put her arms around him, but she couldn't, not with other people in the room.

He didn't return her smile. "This case was supposed to be solved by now."

Allie didn't say anything, so Kyle chimed in.

"You've got to be getting close to solving it, especially with the raven connection."

"Ravens are tricksters," Daniel reminded his Warrior Society friend.

"Maybe the only trick is locating Ann," Kyle responded. "Maybe that's all that needs to be done."

"And the rest will fall into place?" Daniel frowned.

Joyce said, "She fits the profile."

Daniel agreed. "Yes, she does." But it was obvious that the trickster aspect wasn't settling well with him. He locked gazes with Allie again. "I think we should consult Olivia."

"You mean you haven't?" Kyle shook his head. "Why the hell not?"

Daniel answered, "Because Allie doesn't want to worry her sister."

"That's crazy." Kyle put his hand on his wife's tummy. Olivia had predicted the conception of his child long before it happened. "You should call her, Allie."

Damn it, she thought. This wasn't something she'd intended to discuss. "I already talked to her earlier." She'd sneaked in a call that morning.

"You did?" Daniel asked. "What did she say?"

"Nothing. We just wished each other a Merry Christmas."

He frowned once again, a scowl that bracketed his mouth. "You didn't tell her, did you?"

"No, I didn't. I already told you, I'm not ruining her honeymoon."

Daniel snapped. "I'm calling her, Allie. Whether you like it or not."

She argued, "It's eight hours later where she is."

"Too bad." He reached for his cell phone.

Allie glared at the tree. This was turning into a confrontational Christmas, but she couldn't blame Daniel for picking a fight. He was only trying to help. Still, she hated for him to burden her sister. He would probably make it sound worse than it was.

Not that it wasn't bad…

Not that she wasn't afraid…

She grabbed the phone away from him and dialed the number. "I'll tell her myself."

The line rang and rang and Allie almost hung up.

Until Olivia answered. "Hello?"

"Oh, hi, it's me. We just had dinner, and…" She hedged for a moment, hoping her sister would pick up on the troubled vibe.

She did, but who wouldn't? It didn't take an empath to read between the lines. "What's going on? What's wrong?"

"I'm being stalked, threatened, and Daniel thought—"

Olivia's voice jumped. "That I could help? How long has this been going on?"

"A few weeks. We're certain it's a woman. First she trashed my room, then she put ghoulish comics of me on Daniel's door and on his truck." Allie glanced at her lover. He was watching her. "We have a list of suspects, but there's one who's—"

"Mentally ill?" her sister asked quickly.

Allie's pulse jiggered. "Yes."

"Does she have a split personality?"

"She's schizophrenic, but that's not the same as having a dissociative identity disorder." Allie knew because of the research Daniel had done.

"Then my thoughts must be jumbled because that's the feeling I'm getting. But I've been wrong before."

Olivia paused, and Allie pictured her, sitting in a London hotel, with her curious husband by her side. Surely West was locked into the conversation.

"We can come home early," Olivia said. "We can get this figured out together."

"Absolutely not. Daniel and I can handle it on our own. He promised to protect me."

"And you trust him?"

"Yes, of course."

"With your heart?" came the psychic reply. Or maybe it wasn't so psychic. Olivia already knew that Allie was in love with Daniel.

"With my life," Allie said, countering her sister's question. Because trusting Daniel with her heart would hurt far too much.

Chapter 13

Two days later on a dreary Monday morning, Daniel and Allie got ready for work. He'd been dreading this moment, and now it was here.

She glanced out the bedroom window. "They say it's going to rain."

He put on his scrubs, wondering how he was going to concentrate on his job. He'd been keeping in touch with the Kangees, and Ann hadn't returned home, not even for Christmas. "Promise that you'll be careful."

"A little rain never hurt anyone. Besides, it's supposed to clear up by noon."

"You know I wasn't talking about the weather."

"Stop worrying, okay? I'll be fine." She flashed a

brave-hearted smile. "My students wouldn't let anything happen to their favorite teacher."

"Your students are a bunch of elders. What can they do? Fight your stalker off with their canes?"

She swatted his arm. "Very funny."

"I'm serious, Allie. I don't have a good feeling about this."

"The senior center is downtown, with plenty of pedestrians and lots of traffic. I'll be safe there."

"Your loft is downtown, too, and that didn't stop the stalker from trashing it." He stood back and watched her put the finishing touches on her outfit. As always, she wore a gypsy ensemble with Native jewelry. Her hair was long and straight and as dark as a raven's wing.

A raven's wing…

Shaking away the comparison, he moved forward, getting protectively close to her. If he could lock her up in a tower, he would. Like a mythical princess, he thought. Like one of her paintings.

How many times had he imagined her as a character in a fairy tale? Too many, he decided.

Pulling himself back to reality, he said, "I've been thinking about what Olivia said about Ann having a split personality."

"Sometimes my sister's readings aren't accurate."

"I know. But I've been trying to figure it out, to make sense of it, just in case." Olivia was a gifted empath, and he didn't think it was wise to dismiss her input. "Maybe Olivia got that feeling because Ann impersonated you on the day she vandalized your loft. That might make Ann seem like she has dual identities, especially in a psychic's mind."

Allie belted the sash around her waist. "Are you convinced that Ann is the stalker?"

"I'm not convinced of anything." Except that they were being tricked somehow, and that troubled him most of all.

Allie sighed. "Whoever she is, she's dragging it out."

He frowned. "Three threats within two weeks are more than enough."

"I know, but it seems as if we spend most of our time waiting for her to strike again."

We do, he thought, but he didn't respond. Instead, he leaned in to kiss her. She tasted like the lemon-flavored toothpaste she used.

Cool and sexy.

He captured her tongue, and they rubbed against each other. Suddenly he couldn't think beyond his rising erection.

Hungry for more, he backed her against the night-stand until she was seated on the edge of it with her legs open and her skirt hiked up.

"Daniel?"

"We'll make it quick." He removed her panties. "I just need to be inside you."

Allie seemed to need it, too. While he fumbled for a condom, she renewed their lust-driven kiss.

Together, they pulled the front of his scrubs down and the very instant he was sheathed, he plunged into her.

The nightstand rattled, banging against the wall, but the roughness excited both of them. Allie was biting at his lips as they kissed.

Was this what should have happened in the past? Hot sex between friends? Damn, but it felt good.

Still, it was confusing, too.

When the lip-biting ended, he looked into Allie's eyes and thought he saw a secret, something she was keeping to herself.

"Tell me," he said.

"Tell you what?" She slid her hands under his shirt and clawed his back.

"About your secret."

"I don't…"

She clawed him deeper, and he let it go. This was all that should matter. Hot bodies. Feverish sex. Catlike marks on his skin.

He thrust into her again. "You're making me crazy."

She sucked in her breath and wrapped her booted legs around him, pulling him closer, pulling him tighter. Apparently he was making her crazy, too.

Tap. Tap. Tap.

Somewhere in the back of his mind, he heard a hollow sound, then realized the predicted rain had begun to fall.

Big, noisy drops slashed against the window panes, fogging the glass and creating a winter ambience.

He caught Allie's gaze again, and they stared at each other. He was close, so damn close to climaxing.

So was she. He could feel the erotic tremble.

When she gasped and shuddered, he let himself fall into the same carnal abyss. Only now the rain seemed to be inside him.

Pounding wildly against his heart.

On her way to work, Allie reflected on every heated touch, every fast-paced thrust, every spoken word.

Did Daniel suspect that she loved him? Was that what he was asking her to tell him? The secret he wanted her to reveal?

At the time, he'd caught her off guard, and she hadn't understood. But now that she had time to analyze it…

Allie gazed out the windshield. Rain fell in a steady rhythm, and the wipers swished in time to the music on the radio. The oldies station was playing *It Never Rains in Southern California.*

Of course the lyrics weren't meant to be taken literally, and Allie saw them for what they were: an emotional tale, one man's hard-luck journey.

In some ways, the song reminded her of her dad. He'd been a Hollywood actor who'd never really made it.

"I wish you were here, Dad." Then she could confide in him. She could ask for advice, and they could discuss her options.

Should she tell Daniel that she loved him? Should she expose her heart?

Allie arrived at the senior center, her thoughts scattered. But at least she got there in time. Her furniture-rattling romp with Daniel hadn't made her late for work.

She walked from the parking lot to the building, an umbrella overhead. Naturally, she closed it before she went inside.

Allie knew all sorts of superstitions about umbrellas. Never open one indoors. Never give one as a gift. Never place one on your table or bed. Never pick up an umbrella you dropped. Instead, ask someone to do it for you. And finally, if a single woman dropped an umbrella, she would never get married.

The last superstition gave her pause. Allie wanted to get married. She'd always believed in love, in happily ever after, in the white-picket-fence ideal.

She hadn't been tainted, even with a suicide-stricken father and a serial killer mother. Somehow, she'd come out of it with her dreams intact.

Or maybe she was idyllic because of it. Maybe that was the reason she painted fairy tales.

Still gripping her umbrella, she unlocked the art room door and prepared for her students.

As they began to arrive and welcome her back to the classroom, she slipped into her teacher role, grateful for her job.

She taught a variety of classes throughout the day, including drawing, painting, ceramics and pottery.

By lunchtime the rain stopped, and Allie ate in the break room with one of the music teachers.

Later in the day, she analyzed the students in her

final and most advanced class. Some were fussy old souls, and others were bright and happy and bursting with life.

Her most recent enrollee, a widow named Louise Archer, had joined the class a little over a month ago. Louise was one of the most talented artists in the bunch. But she was shy and insecure, too. She rarely met your gaze and ducked her head when you praised her work.

Still, she seemed genuinely nice. She wore thick glasses and thrift store-type clothes. This afternoon, her salt-and-pepper hair was stringy from the rain. Obviously she'd been out in the weather earlier.

Mostly, Louise enjoyed working from live models. But that wasn't today's agenda. Today, they were learning to use color to express mood and emotion. Allie called the lesson, "Painting with Attitude."

Louise appeared to be struggling. Expressing attitude wasn't her thing. But Allie was trying to bring her around, to boost her confidence. She did her best to bond with all of her students.

At the end of the day, Allie was exhausted, but still glad that she'd returned to work.

Later, on her way to the car, she glanced up at the sky. The dark clouds had cleared and there was no need for an umbrella. But Allie held hers tightly, rather than risk dropping it.

Foolish superstitions, she thought. But she couldn't seem to help it.

She approached her vehicle, and her pulse pounded

at her throat. A piece of paper fluttered from beneath the windshield wipers.

Another ghoulish drawing? A threatening note? Had the stalker been here while Allie was in class?

As she got closer, her palms began to sweat.

Then someone called her name.

She spun around and almost dropped her umbrella. Louise was walking toward her. The older woman seemed to come out of nowhere.

Allie just stared at her. A moment later, she caught sight of other cars in the parking lot and realized they had papers beneath their wipers, too. Handbills, she thought. Advertisements. She'd panicked for nothing.

"I have something for you," Louise said.

Allie blinked. "I'm sorry. What?"

"A belated Christmas gift. I didn't want to give it to you in class. Not in front of everyone else." Louise removed a decorative tin from a canvas satchel. "Fruitcake."

Allie smiled. She hated fruitcake, but it was a sweet, old lady thing for Louise to do, so she thanked her kindly. "Did you make it?"

"Yes, I did." Louise spoke softly. "It's a traditional recipe with candied cherries."

Allie accepted the tin. "If you're as good a cook as you are an artist, I'm sure this will be wonderful."

Louise squinted through her glasses. Even now, she wasn't making direct eye contact. She also had a powdery complexion and wore a bit too much rouge. The old-fashioned fruitcake fit her grandma style.

Not that Allie was an authority on grandmas. Her maternal grandmother had been spawned by a long line of witches.

"The class was worried about you while you were gone," Louise said suddenly. "I hope everything is all right."

Allie glanced at the handbills fluttering in the wind. "Everything is fine. I just needed some time off."

"Well, okay, then. I better get going."

"Have a good night."

"You, too."

Louise walked in the direction of the bus stop, and Allie approached her car and removed the paper from the windshield. Sure enough, it was an advertisement.

The stalker hadn't been there.

"Fruitcake," Daniel said when Allie showed him the gift she'd received.

She nodded, trying to appear more relaxed than she felt. She was still debating whether she should tell Daniel that she loved him. But for now, they were sitting on the small patio in his backyard, having a casual conversation.

"Louise seems like a sweet lady," she said. "But I hate fruitcake."

"Really? I like it."

"You do?"

"Yeah." He opened the tin, unwrapped the plastic and broke off a piece.

She watched him pop the icky stuff into his mouth.

"It's good." He took another helping. "Way better than the packaged stuff."

"At least I don't have to lie to Louise now. I can say that my boyfriend enjoyed it."

"Boyfriend?"

Was he amused by the high schoolish tag? She couldn't quite tell. He was eyeing her in a way that seemed to require an explanation.

She said, "I don't think Louise would understand if I called you my friend with benefits. And calling you my lover sounds too sexy to say to one of my students."

"I suppose it does." He closed the fruitcake tin. "I'm so glad your day went well. I was nervous about it."

She decided not to mention the handbills. She didn't want to admit that she'd panicked. Daniel was worried enough. "I like being back at the job."

"I don't. I went stir-crazy today, thinking about you while I was at work."

She wondered if this would be a good time to bring up her secret. If he already suspected that she loved him, then he wouldn't be shocked. He would be ready to discuss it.

Before she could steer the conversation in that direction, he said, "I called Rex earlier and asked him to stop by the senior center tomorrow."

"What for?"

"To talk to the administration and show them a picture of Ann."

Allie scooted forward in her chair. "I don't want my students to know that I'm being stalked. They'll worry." She considered what Louise had told her. "They were already worried about me. They hadn't expected me to take a hasty vacation."

"No one is going to tell them. But I think it's important for the administration to be aware of what's going on."

He was right. How were they going to find Ann if they didn't continue the investigation? She was still the most likely suspect. They hadn't forgotten about Glynis or Susan's sister, but nothing had been pulling them in that direction. Glynis was busy with her chic L.A. life, and Linda was busy with her kids. Lord only knew what Ann was doing.

In the silence, a light breeze blew, stirring leaves on a nearby tree. Daniel used to have a tire swing in the front yard, but he'd taken it down after he'd been released from the hospital, saying it was stupid. Allie used to think it was goofy, too, but now she missed it. Because it was part of the old Daniel, the man with whom she'd first fallen in love.

"Want to go out and get some dinner?" he asked.

"Sure." She drew a quick, shaky breath. "But there's something I think we should discuss."

"Over dinner?"

"No. Now." If she waited, she feared she would lose her nerve. "It's about my secret."

He snared her gaze. "So you *do* have one?"

"Yes, but..."

"But what?"

The intensity in his eyes gave her a quick shiver.

Was this a mistake? Had she spoken too soon? "I assumed you suspected what it was."

He shook his head. "I don't. I just saw something, felt something when we were together this morning, and—" He stalled, and the tension increased. "What is it? What's going on?"

She wanted to say, "Nothing. Never mind," but it was too late for that. Bracing him, she said, "I haven't been totally honest with you."

He frowned, but he didn't respond, making her more nervous.

Finally, she revealed her secret, as steadily as she could. "You're more than a friend to me, Daniel. I'm in love with you, and I have been since you were shot."

He flinched as if he'd just gotten shot all over again. Only this time it was Allie who'd fired the near-fatal bullet.

Chapter 14

Daniel didn't know what to do, what to say. He panicked, all the way to his bones.

But why? What was wrong with being loved by Allie?

"Are you sure?" he asked.

She looked into his eyes. "Why wouldn't I be?"

"Because you said you've loved me since I'd gotten shot. Maybe it's sympathy or guilt or something."

"I know the difference, Daniel. When I was with Raven, I started thinking about you, the way he'd been thinking about his dead wife. We were both confused about our feelings. And then, when you got shot, when you were lying on the museum floor with your shirt stained in blood, I knew that I loved you." She continued to look right at him. "I was so afraid you were going to die."

He was afraid, too. Of losing Allie now. Of not being able to protect her. The Warrior Society was wrong. He wasn't a superhero. He was supposed to be, but he wasn't. With each day that passed, with each day that Allie remained in danger, he cursed himself for not catching her stalker.

"I don't want you to love me," he said.

"I can't help it. I can't make the feeling disappear."

He curled his fingers, closing his hands, struggling to control his emotions. He was torn between taking her in his arms and never touching her again.

"I think you loved me, too," she said. "Before the shooting, before the coma."

Oh, God. Could this get any worse? "What do you mean? You *think?*"

"You never said it. But it seemed like you did. You were really into me."

He still was. But was that the same as loving her? "I can't remember how I felt about you." And he didn't want to think too deeply about the ache that was inside now. "It hurts to love someone."

"It does," she agreed.

"I'm sorry, Allie." He could see how much she was hurting. "But I'd prefer to just be your friend. I can't handle anything more than that."

She finally broke eye contact, and it shattered him to see her looking away.

He tried to explain. "I was hurting when I loved Susan. That much I remember."

She made eye contact again, but not as deeply. There was caution in her voice. "Because she was with another boy and not you?"

He nodded. "Kind of like you and Raven."

"But Raven's gone. He isn't part of my life anymore. There's only you."

How could he tell her that he was afraid of not being able to protect her? He'd failed Susan, hadn't he? The girl he'd loved?

So what did his fear mean? That he loved Allie, too? That he always had? He shook away the thought, not wanting to crowd his already muddled mind.

In addition to his anxiety, he was battling his identity, with being Daniel, with being Fearless. "I just need to focus on the case. To find Ann. To figure out if she's the stalker."

"You were always that way. Driven to succeed. Especially on that last night."

"You mean the museum break-in?" The place where everything had changed, where he'd gotten shot, where Allie had realized that she'd loved him. "How could we have battled supernatural entities? How could we have broken a powerful curse? Yet we can't find the human who's threatening you?"

"Maybe humans are smarter than supernatural beings."

"And maybe we've been overlooking the obvious." He tapped on the fruitcake tin and made a drumlike sound. "Maybe we're not putting the clues together the way we should."

Or maybe they'd gotten sidetracked by their relationship, he thought. The hunger, the need, the fever.

The love.

Flustered, Daniel tugged his hands through his hair, but he might as well be tugging on his amnesiac brain. If anything happened to Allie…

"Maybe you should go away for a while," he said.

"Away from what? You or the stalker?"

"Both. You can go to Europe and stay with your sister and West, and I'll keep working on the case."

But she was stubborn, hanging on to him like a lifeline. "I'm not going anywhere. Not without you."

"You still want to be near me? Even if I'm the reason you're being stalked?"

She set her jaw. "Yes."

He considered sweeping her out of her chair and covering her mouth in a frustrated kiss, but he didn't do it.

She added, "Raven offered me to you."

"What?" He cleared his throat. His pulse was beating triple time.

"He asked you to take care of me. It was an archaic thing for him to do, but he was from another century. He didn't know any different."

"Did I accept the offer?" Daniel asked, even though he knew that he must have. He wouldn't have said no. Not then, and not now.

"Yes, you did."

"So you were given to me? Like a gift?" Itching to touch her, he closed his hands again. "From a warrior who shape-shifted into a trickster?"

She nodded, and he wished that Raven was here to help him keep Allie safe. Or maybe he wanted Raven to teach him how to love her without panicking. That would be a good trick.

"I still can't handle anything beyond friendship," he reiterated.

"It's okay," she responded, her voice cracking a little. "I can handle it for both of us."

Could she? Allie asked herself, as she sat across from Daniel at the Chinese restaurant where they'd gone for dinner. Could she handle it?

Did she have a choice? She loved Daniel too much to let go. But it hurt, dear God, it hurt to be in a one-sided relationship.

Silent, they waited for their food. She'd ordered vegetarian mapo tofu, and he'd ordered orange chicken. For an appetizer, they'd decided on spring rolls, which was something they could share.

Allie was drinking tea, and Daniel swigged on Tsingtao, a brand of Chinese beer. She wondered if she should have gotten alcohol, too. To dull the pain, she thought.

After their waiter delivered the spring rolls, Daniel offered the plate to Allie first. She took one and thanked him, thinking how uncomfortable they were with each other now.

What would it be like later? When they were in bed? How awkward would it be then?

The question stayed on her mind throughout dinner.

Soon their entrees arrived, and while they ate, their conversation remained strained.

At the close of their meal, they reached for their fortune cookies.

"What does yours say?" he asked, filling the silence.

She snapped it in half and removed the slip of paper. Then she stalled, not wanting to read it out loud.

He leaned forward. "Is it bad? Does it say to be beware of something?"

"No." But it was just as disturbing. "It says 'You will always have true and sincere friendship in your life.' "

"Oh, wow. That's weird. Do you think it means us?"

"I don't know." The pain deepened. Being in love with her best friend was getting her nowhere, no matter how true and sincere their friendship was. "What about yours?"

He followed suit and broke his cookie. Soon his expression mirrored hers. He looked troubled by his fortune. "Mine says 'Answer what your heart prompts you.' "

"And what's that?" she asked. "What is your heart prompting?"

"I have no idea." He set the paper aside. "Are you ready to go?"

She nodded, leaving her fortune behind, too.

When they got home, he immersed himself in the

case, researching horror comics on-line and hoping he would discover something that would shed light on the stalker's character and where she might be.

Allie took the lazy way out and watched TV. She couldn't think of anything else to do to keep busy.

At bedtime, things got even more awkward, just as she'd predicted.

"Should I sleep in the guest room?" she asked.

He frowned. "Is that what you want to do?"

"No, but I wasn't sure what I should do."

"You should stay with me, like always."

Okay. Well. Now that they'd settled their sleeping arrangements, she went into the guest room, where she kept her clothes and searched for something to wear, finally deciding on an oversized nightshirt with a ruffled hem. She also put on a pair of lace panties. She returned to Daniel's room. He was wearing boxers.

Allie got into bed first, and he followed. They lay side by side, not talking and not touching.

She was tempted to seduce him, to run her hand along his thigh, to make him hard, but she was afraid of seeming desperate. Using sex in place of love would only make her hurt more.

But honestly, what difference would it make? Hadn't she been doing that already?

She shifted, trying to get comfortable and bumped his arm. "Sorry."

"That's okay." He turned toward her. "It shouldn't be this difficult."

"I know. But it is."

"Maybe I should hold you, like I did before we were lovers."

She couldn't deny him or herself. "That'd be nice, Daniel. Really nice."

He wrapped her in his arms, and she inhaled the fading scent of his cologne. She wanted to cry against his shoulder, but she was too prideful to break down. He stroked a hand down her hair, smoothing the waist-length strands.

"Close your eyes," he whispered.

She did as she was told, much too emotional in his arms. If she wasn't in love with him already, she would have fallen in love with him now. There was no escaping it.

He was, and always would be, the man of her tangled dreams.

In the morning, nothing had changed. The love issue still clung to the air, much like the L.A. smog.

Daniel was in the shower, and all Allie could think about was joining him. Of course she wouldn't dare. Besides, she was already bathed and dressed for work. She'd gotten ready while he'd caught a few hours of early-morning sleep.

Rather than leave Daniel's room, she tidied up, making the bed and fluffing the pillows. But it was a ploy. She wanted to be there when he stepped out of the bathroom with a towel wrapped around his waist and his skin bronzed and damp.

Her timing was perfect. The adjoining bathroom door opened, and there he was.

Gorgeous.

Not only did he look exactly as she'd envisioned him, his gaze latched onto hers. His eyes were an opaque shade of brown, almost the same color as hers. She imagined having babies with him.

One little, two little, three little Indians…

They stared at each other, and she puffed the final pillow.

"You made the bed," he said, stating the obvious. "I would have done it."

"I know." He always made his bed, and he did it with precision. She assumed it was a habit from his military days, even though he barely remembered being in the service. "But I helped muss it up."

"It wasn't that mussed."

Because they hadn't made love, she thought. And she had no right procreating with him in her mind. They weren't a real couple and probably never would be.

"I should get dressed," he said.

"Go ahead," she challenged, the weight of his rejection pressing against her heart.

He angled his head. "You're just going to stand there and watch me?"

"I've seen you naked before."

"Don't tempt me, Allie."

"Tempt you how?"

"How do you think?"

He wanted to touch her. She could see it in his eyes, and she wasn't making it any easier on him.

She gave him a much-needed reprieve and turned away. "I'm going to make some hot tea."

His voice vibrated. He still wanted her. "Will you make me a cup, too?"

She nodded and left the room. She could feel him watching her.

A short time later he joined her in the living room, where she'd set up their tea, along with toast and jam for breakfast.

He sat beside her on the sofa, not too close, but not too far away, either. They both faced the Christmas tree.

"What do you want to do for New Year's eve?" he asked.

"I don't know." The holiday was only days away. "What do you want to do?"

He shrugged and changed the subject. "Don't forget Rex is stopping by the senior center today."

"I remember. How's your work going?"

"Fine. Busy as always."

Today he'd donned tan-colored scrubs and high-top tennis shoes. He used to wear high tops before the coma, too. But he wasn't the same man. The old Daniel would've given into his feelings for her.

Breakfast was short. They munched the toast and finished their tea.

When it was time to leave for work, they stood in the driveway. He lifted his hand as if he meant to touch her, but he dropped it quickly.

"Be good, Allie."

"You, too."

"Call me after Rex gets there."

"I will."

As it turned out, Rex arrived at noon while Allie was on her lunch break. He met up with her after he spoke to the director of the center.

They sat outside in the picnic area. Some of Allie's students were lunching there, along with other seniors whom Allie didn't know. Regardless, she and Rex had chosen a secluded spot.

"Well?" she asked. She couldn't see Rex's eyes or read his expression. He was wearing sunglasses. Unlike yesterday, the weather was warm and dry.

"Ann was here," he responded. "About two months ago. The director remembers giving her a tour of the center. Ann said she was checking it out for her elderly aunt. She was particularly interested in the art department. She claimed her aunt liked to draw."

"Oh, my goodness. That's it. That's why her picture is familiar." Goose bumps broke out along Allie's arms. "Ann visited one of my classes. We get lots of visitors, so it didn't strike me until now."

"As far as the administration knows, she hasn't been back. But they'll be on the lookout for her. They alerted security, too. For all the good that will do."

Allie reacted with a tight nod. Security was an inexperienced rent-a-cop in a uniform.

Distracted, she glanced at the fruit salad and

yogurt she'd brought, but she wasn't hungry anymore. "I promised to call Daniel."

"Tell him I'll be around if he needs me."

"Thanks, Rex."

"Sure thing." He patted her knee before he departed, with his sunglasses still in place.

Allie dialed Daniel on her cell phone, but his voice mail message came on. He was probably assisting in surgery. That was about the only time he wasn't able to answer his phone. She left him a message and told him to call Rex for the details.

After she hung up, she looked around, troubled by her surroundings. The senior center seemed different now.

Ominous, she thought.

Once she returned to her classroom, she felt better.

But was it a false sense of security? She honestly didn't know.

Chapter 15

After the final class of the day ended, Louise asked Allie if she would stay after for a little while to help her with the "Painting with Attitude" lesson.

"I know it's a lot to expect, but I'm having such a hard time with it," the older lady said.

"I don't mind." At this point, Allie needed to be needed. After everything she'd been through, including Daniel's rejection and the knowledge that Ann had stalked her at work, she could use an emotional break.

"Oh, thank you. I felt funny asking, but your classes are really important to me." Louise made a bashful expression. "I have another favor to ask, too. If I stay after, I'll miss my bus. Do you think you could give me a ride home afterward?"

"No problem." Allie didn't mind helping out. "By the way, I wanted to let you that my boyfriend loved the fruitcake."

"Oh, my. Really?" Shy Louise beamed. Then she glanced at the floor, as if she didn't want Allie to catch her looking so happy.

She definitely needed the extra "Painting with Attitude" tutoring. The elderly woman was much too insecure.

Louise lifted her head. "Did you know that I'm part Native American, too?"

"No, I didn't." She'd assumed Louise was some sort of ethnic mix, but with her powdery skin and over-blushed cheeks, her heritage was difficult to define. "Then you definitely need to draw upon your inner warrior and use it in your paintings."

"That sounds fun."

"We'll get started in a minute," Allie said. "I have to make a phone call first."

Leaving Louise at the back of the room, she headed to her desk and removed her purse from the bottom drawer. She retrieved her cell phone, knowing Daniel would want to be informed that she was going to be late. Otherwise, he would worry.

Once she got him on the line, her pulse quickened. Just hearing his voice affected her.

"Did you talk to Rex?" she asked, following up on the P.I.'s visit and the message she'd left for Daniel earlier.

"Yes, I did. Are you okay, Allie?"

She knew he meant emotionally. "I'm fine." She glanced at Louise, who was gazing at a blank canvas. "But I'm going to be a little late. I'm staying after with one of my students. She asked me if I'd give her a ride home, too."

"Which student?"

"Louise Archer."

"The fruitcake lady?"

"Yes." Allie spoke quietly. "She's struggling with our current lesson."

"Will you call me before you head home?"

"Yes, of course."

"Thanks." He paused. "I've been thinking about you all day."

Because of the stalker, she thought. Because he felt responsible for what was happening. "I think about you, too." Because she loved him. Because she feared that he would never return her affection.

"It won't be like this forever," he told her. "Once we find Ann, things will be normal again."

Allie didn't even know what normal was anymore. "I better go." Talking to him wasn't easing the tension. She was actually feeling worse.

"Don't forget to call me later."

"I won't."

They said goodbye and hung up, and she returned to her student.

Louise took one look at her and asked, "Are you all right? You seem upset. Do you want to talk about it?"

Yes, she did. But she couldn't, not without

telling the older woman about the stalker. "Thanks, but I'm fine."

Louise dropped the subject, and they spent a couple of hours on the lesson. Afterward, Allie locked the art room and drove her student home.

She lived in Silver Lake, a district east of Hollywood and known for its eclectic neighborhoods. Her house was small, built in the 1940s, with a rustic porch and positioned on a grassy lot.

"Would you like to come in?" Louise asked. "I can fix some sandwiches."

"Sure." Why not? She'd barely eaten today. Besides, it was a good excuse to stall, to not go home for a while, to avoid the ache of seeing Daniel.

They exited the car and took the stone walkway to the back door.

But once they were inside, someone gave Allie a hard shove and she stumbled to the floor. Before she could recover, she felt a shattering blow to the back of her head.

As the room spun, she called out to Louise, afraid she'd been struck by the intruder, too.

But there was no answer. There was nothing but horrific pain, coupled with the onset of unconsciousness.

Daniel glanced at his watch for what seemed like the hundredth time. Allie was late. She hadn't specified what time she would be home, but that didn't stop him from worrying.

Especially after he called the senior center and learned that Allie and Louise had left hours ago.

The director suggested that she was spending time with Louise at the older woman's home, but when he'd asked for Louise's phone number and address, she'd refused to give it to him. It was against policy to reveal personal information about their students.

He'd pressed the issue, explaining how worried he was that Allie hadn't answered his calls or returned his messages.

Still, the director wouldn't budge. She even asked if Allie might be avoiding him purposely.

Was she? He honestly didn't know.

After he hung up, Daniel dialed 411 and got all of the telephone listings in the Los Angeles area that might be Louise, but none of them panned out. He got on-line and checked national cellular directories, too. But that proved futile, as well. So did the Web sites that claimed they could locate anyone, anywhere.

At his wit's end, he contacted Detective Bell. But it didn't do any good. The police weren't going to search for Allie. According to Bell, the scenario didn't indicate that a crime had been committed against her.

Was Daniel overreacting? Maybe. Regardless, he called Rex and gave the P.I. what little information he had on Louise. To him, she was the key to finding Allie.

Rex agreed and promised to get on it right away.

Daniel ended the call and went outside to wait. He sat on the front stoop and glanced up at the telephone poles, wondering if he would see a raven. Or Raven, he corrected. The Haida demigod.

He came up empty. There were only pigeons and sparrows.

Time ticked by, and as it did, the more frantic he got. He called Allie again and again, but her phone continued to go directly to voice mail.

Maybe she *was* avoiding him. Maybe she couldn't cope with being in love with a man who insisted that friendship was all he could handle.

Daniel made another Raven sweep, but once again, there was no big, black bird.

He cursed out loud, wishing Rex would hurry up and get the information.

Finally, *finally*, the P.I. called.

"I'm having trouble finding a Louise Archer who matches the profile you gave me," Rex told him. "But I'll keep looking."

Impatient, Daniel dragged a hand through his hair. "I think I should give Joyce Prescott a call. She's a cop and a friend of Allie's. I'm sure she'll take this more seriously than Bell."

"Joyce and Kyle are out of town. They went away to celebrate the upcoming New Year."

Well, hell. "Then I'm going to go to the senior center. Maybe the director will be more cooperative in person."

"Good idea. Stay in touch."

"Yeah, you, too." Daniel grabbed his keys and jumped in his truck.

On his way downtown, he battled the ever-present traffic. He finally arrived, grateful the center was still open and the director was working a late shift.

He knocked on her door, and she invited him into her office.

Her name was Madge Sinclair, and she looked to be in her early fifties, about Glynis's age, he supposed. But that was where the similarity ended. She wore her reddish-blond hair in a conservative style and was slightly overweight, with wire-rimmed reading glasses at the end of her nose.

"I'm Daniel Deer Runner," he said.

"Allie's beau? The man on the phone?" She gestured for him to sit. "I'm sorry I wasn't able to help you."

"I understand your position, but what if Allie's stalker followed Allie to Louise's house? Or found a way to kidnap Allie? And maybe Louise, too?"

"If that's what you're afraid of, then why haven't you called the police?"

"I did, but they don't think there's evidence of foul play." He explained further. "All I know is that she was supposed to call me, but she didn't. And no matter how hard I try, I can't reach her. Do you honestly think Louise would mind if you gave me her number? Or better yet, why don't you call her? That wouldn't be against policy, would it?"

"No, it would be okay."

"Then will you do it?"

She nodded, and he sat forward in his chair while

she checked Louise's file on her computer. He should have asked her to this earlier, but he hadn't been thinking straight.

"Oh, dear," she said.

"What's wrong?"

"There's no phone number."

He frowned. "Who doesn't have a phone?"

"People on fixed incomes. People who can't afford one."

"Is there an address?"

"Yes."

"May I have it?" He gazed across the desk. "Please."

She sighed. "If I give it to you, I'm violating our policy. If I don't, I might be putting two women in danger."

"Which do you think is the better choice?"

She wrote down the address and handed it to him.

"Thank you, Ms. Sinclair."

"It's Missus. And I hope I did the right thing."

"You did." He typed the address into the map feature on his phone, but the directions didn't come up. "Something's wrong."

"What do you mean?"

"It says that address doesn't exist."

"Maybe I wrote it down wrong." She double-checked, but she'd been correct the first time. She came up with another theory. "Maybe there's a typo in the computer document. I'll check Louise's original application to see what it says."

Daniel waited while Mrs. Sinclair went to a file

cabinet and rummaged through it. She found the application and placed it on her desk.

"I'm sorry," she said. "But it's the same. Are you sure the map site you used is working properly?"

He tried other sites, but the address didn't exist on them, either. He frowned at his phone. "I don't understand. Why would Louise have given a phony address?"

Mrs. Sinclair had a ready answer. "She could be homeless and is too ashamed to admit it. She could be staying at a shelter."

He countered the director's theory. "If she's ashamed of where she lives, why would she ask Allie to drive her home?"

"I have no idea, but I've seen her at the bus stop, so she must be staying somewhere."

"Do you know what route she takes?"

"No, but I'm sure I can find out."

While Mrs. Sinclair started calling other students in Allie's classes, asking if any of them knew where Louise lived or what bus route she took, Daniel's cell phone rang.

It was Rex. He still hadn't found the right Louise Archer. Daniel told him about the messed-up address, and Rex agreed that something was off.

"Do you have her social security number?" the P.I. asked.

Daniel glanced at Louise's application, which was still on Mrs. Sinclair's desk and repeated the number.

Rex said, "I'll call you back in a few."

Daniel thanked him and walked over to the

window. He glanced out, then saw what he'd been searching for earlier.

A big black bird.

Only it wasn't perched on a telephone wire. It was on the ground in the parking lot, injured or possibly dead.

Like a madman, Daniel took off running, but when he got there, the bird was gone.

Was this a message? Sometimes Raven helped people, even through his trickery. So what did the message mean? That Allie was injured? Or possibly dead?

No, Daniel thought, a lump forming in his chest. Why would Raven appear to him if it was too late to save her?

Once again his cell phone rang, and he glanced quickly at the screen, which identified the caller as Rex.

He flipped open the device. "What'd you find out?"

"Louise's social security number was bogus. Apparently this old woman isn't who she says she is."

As Daniel's thoughts soared, everything that hadn't made sense before now careened through his mind.

Anxious, he gulped a breath. "What if Louise isn't even an old woman?"

"What are you talking about?"

"What if she's Ann?"

Rex was instantly skeptical. "How is that possible?"

"Ann's dad said that she took theater arts and film

classes. And isn't teaching actors how to age themselves part of the basic curriculum?"

"Yes, but that's a far cry from pulling a Mrs. Doubtfire."

"Not if Ann's classes included advanced makeup studies. Besides, she's a skilled artist. She would be really good at it."

"I think you're reaching, Daniel."

"I don't." To him things were starting to fall into place. "Olivia got the feeling that Ann had a split personality. So maybe this is what her reading means."

"That Ann is playing a real-life role? That she's been pretending to be one of Allie's students?" Rex remained skeptical. "Could she actually fool everyone like that?"

"Her name is Kangee. Trickery is in her blood. But it's in mine, too." Daniel told Rex about the message he'd received. *Hoya,* he thought. His mother's clan. "I think Raven is helping me."

Rex didn't dispute Daniel's claim, but he still seemed uncertain about the Ann/Louise connection. "Maybe you should call Detective Bell again."

"I plan on it." But first he went back to Mrs. Sinclair's office.

"Why did you run off like that?" she asked.

He didn't explain that he'd seen a fallen bird. There was no time to educate her about Haida folklore. He queried her instead. "Did you find out what bus route Louise takes?"

She nodded and gave him the information.

He walked away and called Detective Bell, repeating everything he'd told Rex, except the Raven part. Once again, there wasn't time to delve into his culture.

Or maybe he preferred to keep things simple. Somehow he doubted that Bell would acknowledge Native mythology as a means of solving a crime.

The detective responded, "That's quite a theory, Daniel."

He cursed into the phone. Apparently it hadn't mattered that he'd omitted the Raven part. "So that's it? You're not going to help?"

"I didn't say that we wouldn't look into it. I agree that Louise giving the senior center false information is something to consider. Of course there could be a logical explanation."

"Like what?"

"Senility, early Alzheimer's. She might have been having an off day when she filled out her application."

Daniel ignored Bell's logic. To him, there was too much trickery for that. "So what are you going to do?"

"We'll notify the Northeast Division to keep an eye out for Allie's vehicle, particularly in the areas close to Louise's bus route."

Daniel intended to do the same thing. If Allie was at the stalker's house, then her car should be parked there. "I can give you the make and model," he told the detective. "The plate number, too. I've got it memorized."

"Thanks. I figured as much."

At least Bell was willing to help, even if he wasn't convinced that Louise was Ann.

Was Daniel the only person who could see past the deception and comprehended the enormity of the danger Allie was in?

Chapter 16

The bus route spanned at least ten residential miles, and since Daniel didn't know which stop Louise—Ann?—used, he was checking the entire area.

Not only were there single-family homes, there were apartment buildings with underground parking, some of which required electronic openers.

How was he supposed to locate Allie this way? And what about the police? Between them, would they find her?

And if they did, would it be too late?

Daniel kept searching, but he didn't see Allie's car. Where was she? Where was his woman?

His woman?

Did he even have a right to think of her that way?

In the midst of his pursuit, he heard sirens in the near distance.

Once they faded, he sat in his truck, quiet surrounding him. His stomach knotted. Would the emergency detract from the police's effort to find Allie?

Would he be on his own?

He continued his desperate quest. He even went in and out of underground parking structures, following other cars through security gates—a time-consuming exploration that kept him engaged for the next forty minutes.

Time dragged on. Then his cell phone rang.

Detective Bell's voice came on the line. "Where are you, Daniel?"

"In Silver Lake, looking for Allie. Why? What's going on? What happened?"

"We have a hostage situation, and we need to bring you in."

On the outside, Daniel remained calm. Inside, he was shaken to the core: for Allie. The sirens he heard were connected to her.

Bell explained that the Northeast Division had located Allie's car at a residence on Corrin Street, but when they attempted to speak with whoever was inside, a shot was fired at them from the house. No one was hit, but they suspected that they had a hostage situation. Contact was made with the shooter via a cell phone left at the doorstep.

"Is it Ann?" Daniel asked.

"Yes. She claims that she killed Louise and that she intends to kill Allie, too. She refuses to tell the negotiator anything more than that. Since she won't talk to her parents, they haven't been brought in." Bell gave a slight pause. "You're the only one she's willing to talk to. Are you up for it?"

"You know damn well I am."

"Then give me your exact location and we'll send a car."

Daniel recited the information, then asked, "What kind of condition is Allie in? Is she injured?"

"Ann refuses to disclose Allie's condition, other than to say that she's still alive."

The car that quickly appeared was a white vehicle with the LAPD emblem on the sides. Corrin Street was about four miles east of where Daniel was. On the way, he thanked the Creator that the police had found Allie and prayed that she wasn't injured. But he feared that the fallen Raven had indicated otherwise.

Once he arrived at the road-blocked scene, he was immersed in law enforcement procedures. With SWAT teams and sharpshooters in place, with emergency vehicles standing by, he was briefed by Sergeant McGhee, the negotiator in charge.

McGhee looked him straight in the eye. They were about the same height and build, but McGhee was probably twenty years his senior with graying hair and stress-earned lines in his lean, sculpted face.

"Ann won't speak with you on the phone," McGhee said. "She wants to talk to you in person."

"I'm fine with that." Anything to save Allie.

McGhee warned him of the danger. Ann was armed and seemingly confused. Daniel understood. He knew all about Ann's mental illness.

Daniel was given a bulletproof vest. He was wired, too, and fitted with an earpiece to take direction from the negotiator, if necessary.

During the briefing, he was warned that this wasn't a storm-the-castle mission. Daniel's objective was to convince Ann to release the hostage and turn herself in.

"She claims that she already killed the old woman who lives here," McGhee said.

"Detective Bell mentioned that." But Daniel still had his doubts that Louise existed. Or maybe at this point, he was hoping that she wasn't real. He didn't want to envision the fruitcake lady dead on the floor. "Did Bell tell you my theory about the old woman?"

"Yes, he did, and we're looking into who she is. We haven't been able to reach the landlord or locate any documents that verify her identity, but neighbors confirmed that an elderly woman named Louise moved into this house about two months ago. And now Ann Kangee confessed to killing her."

The negotiator got Ann on the phone and told her that Daniel was here. She agreed to meet him on the porch.

The porch was similar to the one at Daniel's dad's

house, and he recalled the day he and Allie had sat in wicker chairs and discussed Christmas decorations.

Most of the houses here were decorated. But this one wasn't. There were no lights, no Santa Claus or reindeers on the lawn.

Across the street was a Nativity scene. That gave him a measure of comfort.

But the neighbors themselves didn't. Unfortunately, not everyone on Corrin Street had been evacuated. Some had gotten trapped in their homes, where they'd been ordered to stay put.

"Ready?" McGhee asked.

Daniel nodded, and once again was reminded of his objective. Were the cops worried that he was going to try to subdue Ann and rescue Allie on his own?

"No heroics," the sergeant said. "Not this time."

This time? Apparently McGhee knew that Daniel had already taken a bullet for Allie and would be willing to do it again if it meant getting her out of this situation.

Regardless, he intended to talk Ann down. He wasn't going to do anything that could backfire and get Allie killed.

"I know what my job is," he said.

"Good." McGhee motioned to the front door, where Ann was peeking her head out.

As Daniel approached her, he could feel the tension that surrounded him. He was glad that Ann's parents weren't here.

He walked onto the porch, and Ann remained where she was.

"It's me," he said to her.

She gave him a cautious perusal and inched out of the doorway, only to duck down behind an old wooden bench that served as porch furniture. She was clutching a junk gun, a compact, inexpensive firearm she'd probably purchased on the streets.

"Do you want me to come back there with you?" he asked, aware of her nervousness.

"Yes," she responded.

The space was tight, but he sat beside her on the floor. Although the slats on the high-backed bench didn't obstruct them from police view, it provided a slight barrier, giving Ann a false sense of security.

She relaxed a little, and Daniel remained mindful of the gun.

"Why don't you let me hold that," he said.

She shook her head, keeping a tight grip on the weapon. Her overall appearance was eerily girlish. She was dressed in jeans, a simple T-shirt and tennis shoes, with her medium-length hair in a bouncy ponytail.

Silent, she watched him through doelike eyes. Her distorted crush on him was palpable, reminding him that Allie was in danger because of him.

He spoke again. "Tell me what I can do to make things better. To fix this."

"You can tell the police to go away. I didn't mean to fire at them. It was an accident."

"It's too late for them to go away. But it's not too late for you to give me the gun."

"But I need it."

"What for?"

"To shoot Allie Whirlwind."

His heart struck his chest. "Why would you want to do that?"

"To give you your memory back." She explained her twisted plan, insisting that Allie was to blame for him changing the style of his hair, for not wearing his glasses anymore, for not remembering that he loved Ann. "If I shoot her at midnight, at the same hour you were shot, it will reverse the process and you'll be the old Daniel again." Still clutching the gun, she added, "I already killed Louise. I tore her face off, and now Allie has to die, too. It's the only way."

He didn't comment about Louise, not yet. But to him, Ann tearing Louise's face off didn't sound like murder. It sounded like the removal of makeup and prosthetics. "Is Allie hurt?"

"A little bit. I hit her over the head and she passed out. Then I put her in bed, gagged her and tied her up. She woke up, but she seems dizzy."

He prayed that Allie hadn't sustained critical damage. He knew how serious head injuries could be.

Was McGhee thinking the same thing? Listening on the other end of the wire and preparing the medics to treat a concussion?

Daniel glanced toward the house. What if Allie developed amnesia? What if *she* lost *her* memory? How horribly ironic would that be?

He turned back to Ann, determined to earn her trust.

"I think you're Louise," he said. "I think you're one and the same. And if you are, then that means that you aren't a killer." He took a chance, reaching out to touch her shoulder, doing what he could to save Allie and get Ann the help she needed.

Distracted by his affection, she almost put the gun down. But then she caught herself. "The voices said that you'd get your memory back after Allie was dead."

The voices in her head, he thought. The schizophrenic blur between fantasy and reality. "What they've been telling you is wrong."

Her eyes turned glassy. "I'm confused."

"I know you are. But it'll be all right. Raven has been guiding me."

She tilted her head. "Raven? Like my name?"

"Yes, and he's more powerful than the voices. He's trying to help you. And Allie, too."

"What about Louise?"

"He wants to help her, too."

"Because he knows I was pretending to be her? I was. But only because the voices said I should."

"You're not a killer, Ann."

"But the voices—"

"It's okay. Just give me the gun, and I'll take you to safety."

"To Raven?" She looked past the porch. "He's with the police."

Daniel didn't see a black bird, but that didn't mean it wasn't present in Ann's delusional mind. Or maybe it actually appeared exclusively for her.

She gulped a shaky breath and turned over the weapon. Daniel made sure the cops knew that he had possession of the gun, and once he and Ann got to their feet, she held on to him.

"Don't forget me," she said. "Don't ever forget me again."

If he hadn't been so emotional, so damn worried about Allie, he would have risked a smile. There was no way he would ever forget Ann, not after all of this.

He guided her down the porch steps and into a throng of police. He gave McGhee the gun and rushed back to the house, SWAT team and medics on his heels.

Allie was in the master bedroom, tied to the bed, mussed and disoriented. But he knew instantly that she recognized him. He could see it in her eyes.

She was confused, but not about him.

At that heart-defining moment, he almost wept. Now he understood how she'd felt at the museum, when he'd been injured and she'd realized that she loved him.

He rode to the hospital with her. In the ambulance, he whispered what she'd been waiting to hear.

"I love you, Allie." He leaned closer. "But I was too afraid to admit it until now. To acknowledge what was happening." Clearly he'd loved her before, the way he'd loved Susan, only more so. "I'm through keeping secrets. From now on, I'm going to express how I feel."

How could he not love Allie? She was his best friend, his lover, the woman who completed the mixed-up man he used to be.

She looked at him, and he suspected that her vision was blurred. But she didn't question his sincerity. She absorbed his declaration like a balm, squeezing his hand and letting him know that she understood every word he'd said.

At the hospital she was kept for observation. Daniel didn't go home. He wasn't about to leave her.

He stayed in a chair beside the bed. And although he'd watched her sleep many times before, this was different.

Because he knew that he loved her.

On New Year's Eve, Allie and Daniel snuggled in bed. Sam was curled up with them, purring quietly. The cat was home, and so was Allie. She was recuperating just fine, but it was too soon to go out on the town. She'd been ordered to rest.

Not that she minded, especially with Daniel by her side. He'd prepared a platter of fruit, cheese and crackers, and they snacked while watching TV, waiting for the ball to drop in Times Square. Instead of drinking champagne, they sipped sparkling cider. Allie wasn't permitted to consume alcohol, not until she was fully recovered.

"Do you think Ann is going to be okay?" she

asked. The troubled young woman was being treated at a psychiatric hospital, rather than being sent to prison. She was in no condition to stand trial.

"She'll always be mentally ill. Her condition isn't curable."

"I know. But I'm hoping she'll go back to the way she was before all this happened. That she won't ever get violent again."

"Most schizophrenics aren't violent."

"I remember Ann's mother saying that. But I guess Ann's prognosis remains to be seen." Allie studied Daniel's profile. "You were the only person who figured out that she was Louise. Even I didn't know, and I was her teacher. Of course now that I look back, I can see the signs I missed. But you know what they say about hindsight."

He turned away from the TV to face her. "I don't know what I would have done if I'd lost you."

"That's how I felt when you'd been shot." She put her hand on his knee. They were looking directly into each other's eyes.

"I'll probably never remember the past," he said. "Other than bits and pieces. But it doesn't matter. We have the future now. We can get married and have kids...." He stalled. "Unless you aren't into that."

"Me?" Her heart pounded. "The happily-ever-after girl? I've already imagined what our kids would look like."

"Really?" He grinned. "Let me guess. Dark hair and dark eyes."

"Yep."

"Sounds logical to me. How many do you want?"

"That depends on how soon we get started."

"Oh, yeah?"

He leaned over to nuzzle her, and she melted into his embrace. She could feel how much he loved her. In his touch, she thought, in the beat of his heart, in every breath he took.

"We'll wait until you're recovered," he said, his voice tickling her ear.

She sighed. "Then I'm going to hurry up and get better."

They separated, and he reached for the platter and fed her a piece of cheese and a couple of green grapes. She fed him, too. It was hopelessly corny. But it was romantic, too.

He toyed with her pajama top, tugging at the material around her tummy. "We'll have to ask your sister to predict what our first baby is going to be."

"Knowing us, it'll be a monkey."

"Or a raven."

"That isn't funny." She scolded him, but they both laughed.

Then she said, "I'm glad Raven was there, Daniel." She meant his Raven, the Haida demigod.

"Yours would have been, too, if he could."

She nodded, grateful that her former lover was safe in the Apache underworld. Of course she and Daniel were safe, as well—in this world, with his Raven to protect them.

Soon the countdown started and they returned to the TV, counting along with it.

At midnight they kissed, and she savored the taste of his lips. For Allie, it was the perfect way to ring in the New Year.

And every year that was still to come.

* * * * *

Celebrate 60 years of pure reading pleasure
with Harlequin®!
Just in time for the holidays,
Silhouette Special Edition®
is proud to present
New York Times *bestselling author*
Kathleen Eagle's
ONE COWBOY, ONE CHRISTMAS

Rodeo rider Zach Beaudry was a travelin' man—until he broke down in middle-of-nowhere South Dakota during a deep freeze. That's when an angel came to his rescue....

"Don't die on me. Come on, Zel. You know how much I love you, girl. You're all I've got. Don't do this to me here. Not *now*."

But Zelda had quit on him, and Zach Beaudry had no one to blame but himself. He'd taken his sweet time hitting the road, and then miscalculated a shortcut. For all he knew he was a hundred miles from gas. But even if they were sitting next to a pump, the ten dollars he had in his pocket wouldn't get him out of South Dakota, which was not where he wanted to be right now. Not even his beloved pickup truck, Zelda, could get him much of anywhere on fumes. He was sitting out in the cold in the middle of nowhere. And getting colder.

He shifted the pickup into Neutral and pulled hard on the steering wheel, using the downhill slope to get her off the blacktop and into the roadside grass, where she shuddered to a standstill. He stroked the padded dash. "You'll be safe here."

But Zach would not. It was getting dark, and it was already too damn cold for his cowboy ass. Zach's battered body was a barometer, and he was feeling South Dakota, big time. He'd have given his right arm to be climbing into a hotel hot tub instead of a brutal blast of north wind. The right was his free arm anyway. Damn thing had lost altitude, touched some part of the bull and caused him a scoreless ride last time out.

It wasn't scoring him a ride this night, either. A carload of teenagers whizzed by, topping off the insult by laying on the horn as they passed him. It was at least twenty minutes before another vehicle came along. He stepped out and waved both arms this time, damn near getting himself killed. Whatever happened to *do unto others?* In places like this, decent people didn't leave each other stranded in the cold.

His face was feeling stiff, and he figured he'd better start walking before his toes went numb. He struck out for a distant yard light, the only sign of human habitation in sight. He couldn't tell how distant, but he knew he'd be hurting by the time he got there, and he was counting on some kindly old man to be answering the door. No shame among the lame.

It wasn't like Zach was fresh off the operating

table—it had been a few months since his last round of repairs—but he hadn't given himself enough time. He'd lopped a couple of weeks off the near end of the doc's estimated recovery time, rigged up a brace, done some heavy-duty taping and climbed onto another bull. Hung in there for five seconds—four seconds past feeling the pop in his hip and three seconds short of the buzzer.

He could still feel the pain shooting down his leg with every step. Only this time he had to pick the damn thing up, swing it forward and drop it down again on his own.

Pride be damned, he just hoped *somebody* would be answering the door at the end of the road. The light in the front window was a good sign.

The four steps to the covered porch might as well have been four hundred, and he was looking to climb them with a lead weight chained to his left leg. His eyes were just as screwed up as his hip. Big black spots danced around with tiny red flashers, and he couldn't tell what was real and what wasn't. He stumbled over some shrubbery, steadied himself on the porch railing and peered between vertical slats.

There in the front window stood a spruce tree with a silver star affixed to the top. Zach was pretty sure the red sparks were all in his head, but the white lights twinkling by the hundreds throughout the huge tree, those were real. He wasn't too sure about the woman hanging the shiny balls. Most of her hair was caught up on her head and fastened in a curly clump, but the light captured by the escaped bits crowned her with a golden halo. Her face was a soft shadow, her body a willowy silhouette beneath a long white gown. If this was where the mind ran off to when cold started shutting down the rest of the body, then Zach's final worldly thought was, *This ain't such a bad way to go.*

If she would just turn to the window, he could die looking into the eyes of a Christmas angel.

* * * * *

Could this woman from Zach's past get the lonesome cowboy to come in from the cold... for good? Look for ONE COWBOY, ONE CHRISTMAS by Kathleen Eagle Available December 2009 from Silhouette Special Edition®

COMING NEXT MONTH

Available November 24, 2009

#1587 THE CAVANAUGH CODE—Marie Ferrarella
Cavanaugh Justice
When detective Taylor McIntyre discovers a suspicious man lurking around a crime scene, she never guesses he'll be her new partner on the case. But the moment J. C. Laredo sweeps into the squad room, Taylor can't deny the attraction she feels for the P.I. As they work the nights aw growing ever closer to catching the killer, will they finally give in to the love that's been building inside?

#1588 THE SOLDIER'S SECRET DAUGHTER—Cindy Dees
Top Secret Deliveries
Her mystery man disappeared after their one night of passion, but he left Emily Grainger with a constant reminder—their daughter. So when she receives a tip that leads her to a ship's container, she's shocked to discov her long-lost love held captive inside! Now on the run from his captors, Jagger Holtz will do anything to protect his newly discovered family.

#1589 SEDUCED BY THE OPERATIVE—Merline Lovelace
Code Name: Danger
The president's daughter is having strange dreams, and psychologist Claire Cantwell has been tasked with finding their cause. In a desperate race against time, she and Colonel Luis Esteban follow a mysterious trail halfway around the world. As they face a lethal killer, can they also learn to face their own demons and give in to the love they clearly feel for each other?

#1590 PROTECTING THEIR BABY—Sheri WhiteFeather
Warrior Society
After her first and only one-night stand, Lisa Gordon suddenly finds herself pregnant...and in danger. Rex Sixkiller enjoys his free-spirited lif but when Lisa and his unborn child are threatened, he takes action. As th threats escalate and Rex fights to keep them safe, he and Lisa also wage losing battle to protect their hearts.

SRSCNMBPA110